# BUD'S LOVE BUS

Raz Cue

Bud's Love Bus, "420 Bus" concept & design by Raz Cue

Illustration by Doug Millhoff

Copy Editing: Nathan DelaCastro

ISBN-10 0982710305

ISBN-13 9780982710302

FIRST REVISED EDITION 2017

©2008-2017 Stoneweed Press
Las Vegas, NV
Stoneweedpress.com

Thanks to the shut-ins and outcasts, as well as some fairly normal folks, in my writers' group. Especially Mandy and Chelsea, but I still have lots of love for Gordon, Rachel, Chris, J.J., Zeenat, Hilary, Katie, Paul, Aileen & Bill, Tanya, Greg, Susan and Elizabeth. Plus anyone else who occasionally dropped in and read my shit to help polish it into this turd currently leaving stank upon your fingertips! Last but not least, a big shout-out to Maxwell Alexander Drake whose writing classes provided uncountable aha moments.

*Drugs: Don't try them. You might like them!*

# Visit Budslovebus.com
# for the Sweetest Swag
# South of Saskatchewan!!!

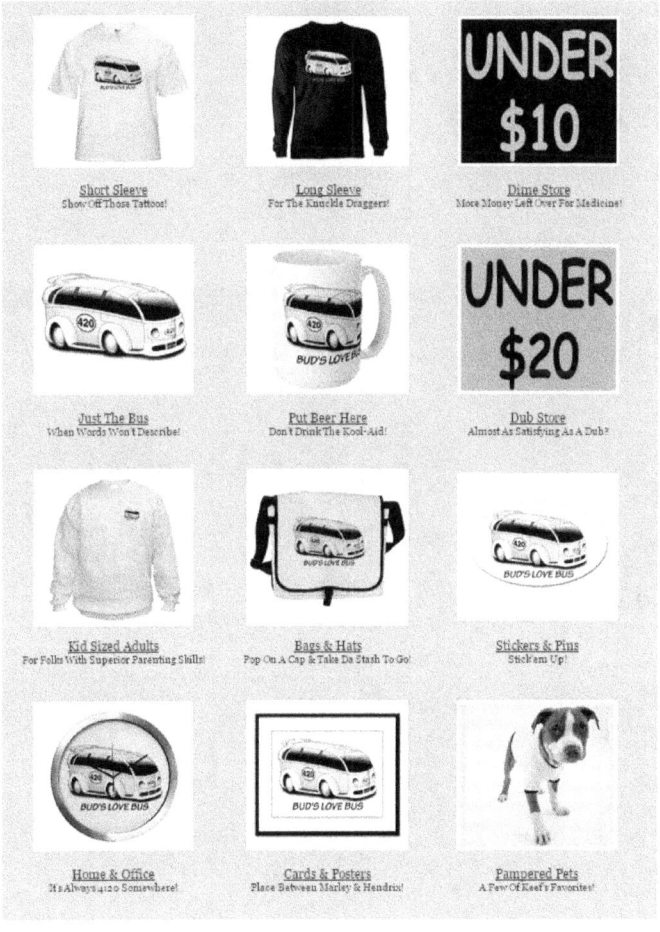

Also Sign Up To Receive **FREE** Prizes
& Deep Discounts on Bud Gear!

# 1

*North Hollywood, California*

On a moonless midnight, about a year before the war on drugs ended with a whimper, Herb Gardener pleaded, "Please, no sidetracks or titty bars. Just get those drives and head straight home."

Conveying the confidence of one who seldom fails, Frank Odious sat at the wheel of his utterly balls-out-badass Victory Red Corvette, waiting patiently for the go signal.

To his right, Bud Green, suckling an ever present super-sized doobie, wore his usual dopey grin.

Herb stood alongside the passenger door and, with his trademark whine, repeated for the umpteenth time, "In six hours my cousin's leaving for a three-day fishing trip. If I don't have another drive by tonight, the Love Bus will never be ready by the deadline."

Bud's face revealed no evidence of concern as he passed the joint. "We got plenty of time, bro."

Herb took a toke while handing back a Ziploc baggie half filled with colorful, rich, and vibrant weed. "Careful with that," he warned. "It's 'The Plague.' Give it to my cuz – AFTER he gives you my drives!"

"Right on," Bud said, stashing the baggie in an oversized cargo pocket. In one sweeping motion, he stuck his arm straight ahead and said, "Hit it, bro!"

Frank's smile grew wider than the ass of a Sir Mix-A-Lot backup dancer as he bellowed, "W-a-a-a-h-h-h-gun-s-s ho-oh!" A twist of the key brought that muscle-car roaring to life with a rumble that sounded like World War Eleven. With an outstretched middle finger, he bid a fond farewell to Herb and slapped the car into gear, doing a brake-stand until the motor screamed past 5,000 RPM and then, in a blur, the Vette slingshotted from the lot like an F-35 off an aircraft carrier's deck, leaving its path recorded in seared Goodyear rubber halfway up the block.

Twelve point three seconds later, Frank pulled a hard left and the Vette's rear wheels broke free into a drift until the nose lined up to the on-ramp and he mashed the accelerator to the floor while screaming, "Yeeeeee-Haaaaaaw!" With a bounce and shimmy, the motorized muscle beast returned to a laser-straight path toward destiny.

Bud, face pale, hand strangling the armrest, pressed so deep into the seat he was damn near in the backseat, disguised his begging as best he could. "We got six hours to get there, and it's only four hours away. If we get pulled over, we're screwed."

"Okay," said Frank while easing ever so slightly off the pedal. "But I want to get there – titties and beer – and back by dinner tonight."

Bud's tension melted away in concert with deceleration and he rediscovered his smile muscles. "Right on," he said. When his breathing returned to near normal, he retrieved their next doobie from his duffle bag.

Two hours, one hundred seventy-eight miles, and three joints later, the guys enjoyed Corvette's version of the leisurely drive whilst they spoke of normal things.

"They should change the name of Vegas to, 'I should have fucking left,'" Frank chuckled.

Bud gave a full-throated, "Viva Lost Wages!"

After joining in for a chorus and a half, Frank passed along a fun fact. "I read that only 15 percent of shark attacks on humans are fatal."

Bud shrugged. "Wow, you'd think it'd be more than that."

"Yep, it's true," Frank said. "Most shark attacks are just a single bite. I'm thinking it's probably because sharks feel along with their teeth."

"Or maybe humans taste like crap?"

"Speak for yourself, bro. Because I am one delicious motherfucker." Frank grinned. "It ain't just your momma who thinks so, either!"

Bud made the mistake of picturing the scenario, followed by a shudder within a shudder, accompanied by an almost dry-heave mini gag. "Dude, that's fuckin' gross. But listen, it all makes sense. If humans tasted good, there'd be way more cannibalism going on. Why go out in the woods to hunt for food if you've got tasty neighbors?"

"You might be right," Frank said. "Maybe if we asked a cannibal about feasts of friend, we'd find out that 'people definitely don't taste like chicken.'"

Bud stared ahead, mesmerized by the road's white lines seemingly melting into one.

Four minutes later, he said, "Why do they always say stuff tastes like chicken?"

"I don't know," said Frank. "But I ate some chicken the other day, and strangely enough – it too tasted just like chicken."

An hour later, gliding along the smooth, arrow-straight highway, they flew past a CHP officer delivering a citation to another hurried motorist. As they flashed by, Bud looked right at the officer and the officer looked straight at the smoking bomber hanging from his lips.

Bud blurted out the vital information, "Shit, cop, bro!"

Frank's eyes darted to rearview as he attempted to stomp the accelerator through the floorboard. "Did he notice us?"

"Oh yeah, he sure did," Bud said. "He's running for his car."

"Fuck," said Frank.

Bud craned his neck back to seek the latest information. "He's almost back to it."

A minute later, Frank's expression and focus were not unlike someone engrossed in a beloved action movie. Both white-knuckled hands tightly gripped the wheel and, with eyes open wider than the muscle car's throttle, he spoke appreciatively, "Damn, this fucking car really moves! I never hit top speed before."

The CHP cruiser was a bad motherfucker, too. Trailing more than a mile back, the menacing flashing red lights gamely kept pace with the guys.

Frank kept his eyeballs Super Glued to the asphalt ahead, watching for curves, bumps, slower traffic, or any other sign that the end was nigh. They didn't have to wait long – things happen fast in Corvettes.

Straight ahead, freedom's path was blocked by two cars traveling right at the posted speed limit, inexplicably side by side along the deserted midnight two-lane highway.

Reluctantly, and ever so slightly, Frank backed off the gas to shave off a few MPH. The mirror's flashing red lights grew at an alarming rate, so he mashed the horn to sound an alarm of collective fates aggressively converging on collective doom.

Frank's eyes darted back and forth from mirror to road while in a hushed mumble he repeated, "Shit-fuck, shit-fuck..."

While repeatedly slam-tapping balled fist on the armrest harder and harder, Bud panic-grumbled, "C'mon c'mon c'mon c'mon c'mon – move, motherfucker!" and then he bellowed, "GET OUT OF THE WAY, MORON! THE LEFT LANE IS FOR PASSING!"

Not two full seconds later, decisive action begged hungrily for its opportunity to shine. With red flashing lights overtaking his mirror, Frank eased left and was greeted by a *THUD THUD THUD THUD* from the road shoulder's rumble strips' deliverance dirge methodically rattling their high-tech death sled.

Just shy of a split second later, more than a hundred yards past the immediate concern and on to the next, Frank jerked the wheel to redirect his steed toward smooth, middle-of-the-road safety and the Vette launched Heavenward. Ascension was rejected by angels above when gravity's black magic pulled them back to earth with a shimmy and a bounce. Each touchdown sent a shower of brilliant sparks crackling like a thousand fireflies into the pitch-black night.

As they flew on down the highway, Frank smiled and freed up a hand for a high-five. "That was awesome!"

Having lost the ability to vocalize, Bud offered an imperceptible nod while battling an urge to defecate.

The red lights shrunk smaller and then smaller. Then they disappeared.

Ten minutes later, for the ninetieth time Frank sought reassurance and comfort from his rearview mirror and for the fortieth time said, "I think I lost him."

Nevertheless, he stayed heavy on the throttle.

Miles down the highway, the unforgiving physics of serpentine mountain roads compelled him to slow down to a hundred ten, and then Frank whooped and yahooed his way to the top of the mountain.

At the mountain's crest, the Vette came out of a sweeping left turn to begin her hurried descent toward the cluster of twinkling lights tearing a hole through distant blackness.

Bud said, "I think we can slow down a bit now. Please."

"Sure, dude." Frank nodded while backing that bitch down.

On down the road a piece, the rearview mirror relayed alarming information, which Frank passed along. "Shit, there's a fucking red light flashing way back there."

Bud's fingernails found their way back into their previous imprints, "Step on it, bro."

Frank was on it in a flash. He pointed ahead to the little city's bright lights. "That's the state line. If everything stays cool, in two minutes the only thing we'll have to worry about is the Nevada Highway Patrol, or some exotic dancer's angry, unemployed boyfriend."

"And crashing," said Bud.

"That would be un-cool, so I think I covered that. As I was saying, if we…"

The engine's sudden silence unceremoniously changed that plan. Very un-cool.

"Fuck, we're out of gas," Frank said. Dejected by the buzz of joyous thrill being snatched away only makes the letdown that much more intense, and he spoke in a sad whisper, "We're fucked, now."

Bud hijacked the melancholy with a new plan of action. "Turn off the lights and put it in neutral," he commanded. "Let's see if momentum will roll this bad-boy into Nevada. Don't use the brakes or the lights will go on; might as well just honk and wave at that cop."

Something ultra-rare and unexpected occurred; Frank did as he was told.

A sliver of merciful sun peaked over the eastern horizon, casting just enough light to almost make the road visible.

The mirrors' flashing red lights grew at an alarming rate, but the Vette still advanced swiftly enough that crossing the state line before getting nabbed was not an unreasonable assumption.

"If we can make it to the top of the ramp, we might be able to sweep right and roll through the light," Bud said. "Maybe get gas somehow, or hit McDonald's and blend in with the crowd."

"I don't know." Frank's eyes darted from mirror to hope-we-can and back several times. "But I guess it's our best shot."

As if a CHP cruiser closing in fast from behind wasn't enough, on the other side of the road the flashing lights of an approaching Nevada law enforcement vehicle did not sow confidence that liberty would be anything more than short lived.

Upon crossing the state line, the car still possessed enough fight in her to make the top of the off-ramp, where Frank pulled a long, sweeping right turn through the intersection and got almost to the next light, but not quite.

Before the Vette's forward progress ceased altogether, Frank barked, "Get out and push this fucker!"

The two sprang from their seats like feral cats from a tub of water then trotted alongside the car, steering, pushing, and hyperventilating.

At the stoplight, Frank pushed the wheel right. Around the corner, they came upon a mini-market gas station, empty except for an old colorfully painted school bus parked at the first pump.

Frank shouted, "Quick, into the truck stop."

"Are we gonna get gas?"

Frank said, "Do I look like a fucking psychic?"

Mere feet shy of the gas station, the flickering red reflection emanating from the highway's direction bounced and danced upon the Vette's windows. Red flashing lights have a way of hastening the pace and focus of wanted men, so Frank yelled, "Change of plans, bro – nowhere to hide in there."

Frank yanked the steering wheel hard left, and yelled, "Let's get her between those two big rigs across the street. Step on it, dude!"

Seconds later, Frank jumped behind the wheel and guided the car between two semi tractor trailers and yanked the emergency brake before bolting from the cockpit to join Bud and update their evolving flight plan.

Bud, hands on knees, huffed and puffed and asked, "Now what, McDonald's?"

The ancient school bus from the gas station appeared, creaked and groaned, and then backed up toward them before Frank could catch his breath to answer. Its rear bumper stopped a few feet shy of the Vette and went dark at the exact instant the engine quit rattling and its tailpipe released a final sigh.

In an instant, the guys were very well hidden.

Frank put on his best shit-eating-grin and gave a triumphant fist pump. "That's what, bitch."

"Just like you planned it, huh, fucker?" Bud said.

Bud spun in a tight little circle, examining the semi-trailer-walled enclosure and the school bus's backside corking it all up. "Dude, this is too weird. Maybe we crashed and burned. This could be the afterlife."

Frank waved an arm like a game show model. "This ain't the afterlife. It's Primm, Nevada!"

With a morbid moan, the old bus's long un-oiled door swung outward, narrowly missing knocking Bud's noggin. An old, smiley, hairy, hippie-looking head emerged from within and spoke some gibberish. "Can Duke park a bus or what? I tell you it's all about them spatial relations. Either you got 'em or you don't. And he's got 'em."

Frank glanced to and fro, nodded, and agreed, "I wouldn't have thought that bus would have fit in here."

Bud shrugged. "I guess."

"Greetings, friends. I'm Raoul. Just a wild guess, but you two must be the little red Corvette we heard about on the radio. Looks like we arrived right on time. Need a lift?"

"Hell yes!" Frank and Bud blurted in stereo.

"Hop in then. But be quick."

They started toward the happy, helpful hippie.

In the blink of an eye, Raoul's cheerful expression flipped to one of serious concern. "Oh yeah, I hope you kids don't mind, but Duke and me been smoking marijuana. I assure you, strictly for medicinal purposes."

"No problem, man." Frank sprang aboard. "That's more than groovy with us."

Bud nodded and boarded in one fell swoop.

When they were just barely past the portal, Raoul slammed the door behind them. In an instant, the bus engine began chugging and churning in futile protest of its forced awakening, but gave in and rattled to life with a slightly off-tempo cadence to transport the foursome forward.

The driver barked into his CB's microphone, "Now, good buddy, over!"

Three seconds later, an eighteen wheeler rolled backward past the bus and into its vacated spot, once again shielding the Vette from prying eyes.

With a friendly grin on his whiskered face, Raoul surveyed the scene unfolding through the rear window. "That'll buy you kids some time."

As the bus inched forward like a turtle crawling on arthritic elbows, they all settled in near the front.

"Hola, kids, I'm Duke," said the driver.

Both of the old guys looked like a cross between Willie Nelson and Chuck Manson dressed the same, but different, with neither smelling any worse than the other. Thankfully the graceful remnants of musk and patchouli incense permeating the immediate space overtook any olfactory objection.

Crouched low and peeking from behind tapestry-laden bench seats, Frank and Bud introduced themselves in low tones.

"Looky ahead there, folks." Duke gave a slight nod toward two law enforcement vehicles, driver's side door to door with plumes of steam belching from their rattling tail pipes.

The officers passionately jawed with one another amongst the red and blue lightshow bouncing off underpass walls while Frank and Bud tried to crawl under the floor.

Enough said; the cruisers sprang forward like jackrabbits with an aversion to providing nourishment for higher mammals.

The NHP cruiser jetted past the bus in the direction of a certain abandoned Corvette.

The CHP cruiser hung a left at the westbound on-ramp and shot off like a cannon blast toward Baker.

Duke chose a third option, directing the rolling relic toward Sin City.

No one felt any responsibility to get a conversation started, choosing to focus on the road ahead and the sun's relentless rise. Engulfed in silence and dissipating adrenaline, they puttered along slightly faster than a moped with a fouled sparkplug being ridden up a steep grade by an obese couple.

The group's contemplation and decompression ended abruptly when, out of the blue, Frank whooped, "What a rush!"

He reached over to high-five Bud, who left him hanging.

Frank caught Dukes' glance from the mirror, and he patted Raoul on the shoulder. "And you guys, thanks a million. We owe you big time. No doubt about it!"

Bud managed a slow nod before allowing himself an ever-so-slight smile. "Yeah, thanks guys." After a heaving sigh, an even bigger smile overtook the first. "Frank's right. We owe you more than we can ever repay."

"You're welcome," said Raoul. "But don't be silly, kids."

"I hope this doesn't come out wrong," Bud said, "but why did you guys go to all that hassle to save us?"

"We heard of your troubles on the radio, just as we were finishing up meeting a client at the rest area," Duke said. "We were bored, so we decided to see if we could help."

"And because we hate pigs," Raoul said.

Duke nodded.

"It's all good, and thanks," Bud said. "Except for them always trying to bust me for weed, I love cops."

"I love that we made a clean getaway," Frank said.

"Before you get too excited, let's check in with our trucker buddy with eyes on that bubblegum machine," Raoul said.

With eyes fixed ahead, Duke keyed the CB mic and spoke forcefully, "Gonzo Gang here, you read me, Mother Trucker? Come in, Mother Trucker."

Quicker than butter melting on hot toast, the CB's speaker crackled a reply. "Mother Trucker here – bring it back to me, Gonzo."

"Right on," said Duke. "Gracias, amigo, on the park in the dark hide the ride. What's the four-one-one, over?"

"Car is out of sight like midnight delight. Bring it back," squawked Mother Trucker.

"Roger that," said Duke. "Whiskey-Tango-Fox is the goings-on at the state line, over?"

"It's one great big Smokey party at my twenty, good buddy," Trucker said. "There's more bubblegum here than a top-forty radio show. Them bears is snooping around like an old hound dog sniffin' for a bone, bring it back."

"Thanks, good buddy," Duke said. "If Smokey gets eyeballs on the roller skate's ninety-nine, y'all holler a nine-one-one, over."

"That's a big ten-four," Trucker said. "Over and out."

Duke, refusing to take his eyes off the road, fumbled about to secure the mic in its cradle.

"Can you trust that Mother Trucker?" Bud asked.

"Sure, known Mother for years," Duke said. "We do a wee bit o' business with him every few weeks. Mobile sign painting and herbal remedies is our trade."

Raoul smiled. "Would you kids dig smoking some grass?"

Bud perked up. In a flash, all the night's events no longer seemed to matter. "Always – spark it!"

Moments later, the foursome were sharing common interests as a multi-generational hemp-haze rose lazily while twisting and swirling within itself.

Raoul gestured ahead. "You kids heading to Vegas to party?"

"Business," Frank said. "We've been working nonstop for months building a car, and in just two days we have the unveiling scheduled for a whole slew of big wigs." With rolling eyes, he gestured toward Bud. "Someone lost some do-or-die critical parts."

"It's not that big a deal." Bud shrugged. "We located some replacements in Vegas. All we got to do is pick 'em up and everyone should quit bitching at me."

"You kids restoring a car?" said Duke.

"Not exactly," Bud said. "We built an alternative fuel vehicle from the ground up."

"It runs on weed," Frank said. "But the best thing is, it gets a thousand miles per ounce."

Raoul let out a long, slow whistle. "Amazing," he said. "If it's true, that's beautiful, and a great relief for Mother Earth."

"It was all our friend Herb's idea," Frank said. "He did all the technical design. Bud and I just put it all together."

Bud's teeth clenched while he fought an urge to correct the record. Instead of opening a can of who cares, he changed subjects. "Well, I designed and built the BongRiteEndlessHigh."

"What's that?" Duke said.

"It's basically just an automatic bong," Frank said.

"Right on," said Duke. "But can I ask you kids another question?"

Bud passed him the ever-shrinking joint. "Go ahead."

Duke took a respectable pull, paused, passed, then pondered until once again pride lost a short yet intense battle to curiosity. "What is, did you say, 'a-bong?'"

Bud chuckled, not condescending, more akin to a joke shared amongst old friends. "Yup, it's a water pipe."

Frank said, "Wow, you dudes don't get out much, do you?"

Two jolly relics of daze-gone-by shook their heads in unison.

Frank seldom let an opportunity for a bullshit session slip away, so he said, "So you haven't heard that Abbie Hoffman and Patty Hearst got married? They're building a nuclear power plant right up the coast from where their fleet of whaling ships dock."

Duke was the only one that didn't laugh, his focus occupied by concern about the road ahead. "We really should get off the main highway before the sun comes up more. We'll lay low a few hours, and by then it should be safe to head back to Primm."

The last syllable of Duke's plan hung in the air as the CB's speaker crackled to life. "Mother Trucker to Gonzo Gang, you copy?"

Duke won a brief, energetic battle with the microphone's cradle. "Gonzo Gang here, read you loud and clear, Mother. Bring back the news, good buddy."

The reply's delay, in reality mere seconds wrapped in anticipation's cloak of expected disaster, felt like forever.

"Copy that, Gonzo Gang," Trucker said. "Smokey left for his cave. Now we got less pork than a Jewish wedding at my twenty. Bring it back."

"Thanks for the four-one-one, Mother," Duke said. "Follow the lights home, over."

"Catch you next time at the pickle park," Trucker said. "Over and out."

Raoul saved his friend a bit of aggravation by snatching the mic away and clicking it home.

Duke said, "Looks like we can ride you kids back to Primm now."

"Yeah, about that," Bud said. "We got to be at the parts place in less than two hours, and we'll never make Primm and then back to Vegas in time."

"We're kinda hoping that you guys will ride us there," Frank said. "We'll make it worth your while."

Raoul shrugged. "Whaddya think, Duke?"

Duke glanced up at Frank and Bud pantomime-begging in the rearview mirror, smiled, and nodded. "We can do that."

"You two are the best," said Bud.

Frank grinned. "Say, either of you two ever smoked any hydro-bud?"

"What's that?" asked Duke.

"It's grass, dummy," said Raoul.

With a hippy-go-lucky smile, like the one often found on cartoon lizards offering sage advice as you wander the desert tripping balls on mushrooms, Duke said, "Right on. Light it up!"

"It's a couple of notches above that grass stuff," Bud chuckled. "But it's all good."

"Watch out, old-timers," Frank warned. "Get ready for the bomb-shit, because this 'grass' is like a B-52 raid on your brain."

The two ever-smiling hippies nodded, offering no resistance to exploration of new weed things.

Bud retrieved a party bomb from deep within his duffle, which he then proudly displayed for all to admire. "Here it is, folks."

"Wow, that's got to be the biggest joint I've ever seen," Raoul said.

Curiosity got the better of Duke, causing him to peel his eyes from the road. "Yeah, far out, man." Quicker than the flap of a hummingbird's wings, he returned his attention straight ahead.

Bud sparked it up, and then puffed until a bright red cherry glowed. After an exceptional pull or three, he passed it to Raoul who eagerly received the spliff.

Almost finished inhaling, Raoul's lungs buckled, causing him to cough like an asthmatic monkey engulfed in a searing cyanide-methane cloud. With tears leaking from burning eyes, his pulmonary distress continued far longer than an extended moment before THC began dancing a jig on his brain. He smiled. "Far out, man."

While everyone cracked up, Raoul seized the opportunity to once again starve his brain of oxygen. His second hit was attacked with diligent caution, which allowed for a far less traumatic exhale of the candy-sweet smoke.

"That grass smells magically delicious," Duke said. "Don't bogart that joint, man."

A few hefty puffs later, Duke laughed, chuckle-laughed, looked around for some chips, took another puff, and then asked, "Did you guys really build a car that runs on weed? How does it work?"

# 2

Six months earlier, the genesis of the Love Bus project began quite innocently within the confines of a warehouse where Bud and Herb lived, worked, smoked, and smoked. And smoked. The work involved maintaining a thriving cannabis cultivation operation, which took up the lion's share of the nondescript ten-thousand-square-foot concrete block building. The remaining space provided more than ample living and work space, and at times enough legroom for a little street skating or WWE-style roughhousing. Herb owned the joint, purchased with money left to him by a wealthy uncle, and often reminded those who disagreed with him – Bud – of that fact. The reason he bought such a huge building – besides Herb being a salesman's dream – was that he wanted lots of space for tinkering on experiments and inventions in hopes of brainstorming up a billion-dollar idea. Unfortunately, after a few years of maintenance, taxes, utilities, and materials, his funds had nearly evaporated before he'd discovered even a hundred-dollar idea.

Soon after Herb had the property's title in hand, Frank and Bud began their relentless pestering, trying to convince him to cultivate "medical marijuana" in the vast unused space right outside his workshop's door. Herb, afraid of getting busted, repeatedly refused. Relaxed marijuana laws and an urgent need for a cash infusion ultimately convinced him to get growing.

With the green light shining bright, Frank and Bud hit the gas and immediately began raising walls to create cultivation spaces. Frank whelt and dealt and bartered and charmed and flirted to single-handedly score most of the needed electronics and hydroponic equipment. When he came in and saw the stacks of free equipment, Herb was so absolutely thrilled that he made Frank an equal partner; equal to Bud, because Herb got half. Within a month, the first clones were loving life in their nourishing hydroponic soup while basking in luxurious artificial sunlight. By the end of six months, the pile of buds halfway to Stoner Heaven made it all seem like something so right.

Three years in, they were all doing way better than just "making a living." Life's only bummer was Herb's aversion to any prolonged contentment. Frank and Bud often tried soothing Herb's dour disposition by pointing out that "technically" they were all in "the medical profession" and his "mother would be proud." Try as they might to cheer him up, it wouldn't fly, because Herb wanted "more from life than being a drug dealer."

That particular day, when the Love Bus project was birthed, Bud stomped into the kickback area, arms flailing wildly about like some air-filled creature sitting on the curb out front of a shady used car lot, and at high volume complained, "Man, I can't believe these fuckin' gas prices. What a load of crap! Who in the hell can afford that shit? We need to bomb someone back to the Stone Age; that'll drive them fuckin' prices down."

Herb kept his head down, fighting the urge to peel himself from his book. He knew better than to comment if he wanted to continue reading. But self-righteous disgust once again motivated him to dart those angry beady eyes toward Bud and berate him like one does a young child with their Sunday best covered in mud. "You have said plenty of idiotic shit over the years, but that has got to be the most foolish and evil statement ever uttered from your idiotic trap. America cannot go around bombing oil-producing nations just because the cost of gasoline rises."

"Who said anything about an oil-producing nation?" Bud shrugged. "I meant that to let off a wee bit o' steam we could bomb Canada or something. Lob a few SAMs over Niagara Falls, so them mutha-Canuckers from the Great White North won't ever again mistake our neighborly kindness for weakness, ay."

Like a parent who just found out their child ran off with a circus, Herb snapped at the clown before him, "Have you been seeking wisdom from the Oracle of Doo-Phi again?"

Bud tried to fight it, but a goofy grin betrayed him once again. "I learnt a bunch of shit from Frank," he giggled. "But just like you, he's lucky if he's right half the time."

"Too bad you two aren't in charge," Herb snarled. "For your information, Canada is our closest ally, and by far our number one supplier of crude oil. Have I told you lately what a fucking moron you are?"

"I'm more-on than I'm off, fucker." Bud did a little soft shoe shuffle.

Herb scowled. "You are a complete idiot."

"It takes a village to raise an idiot," said Bud.

For a moment it seemed like Herb would let it slide. Instead, he drew a deep breath and then took far too long to expel all that hot air. "Let's get back to the high price of gasoline."

Bud, figuring that it was over, had saddled up on the couch to greet his bong, so he just nodded and mumbled, "Yeah, that shit sucks big ol' donkey dicks."

"It sucks on many levels," Herb said, "price being the least important of those issues."

Bud thought for a moment. But try as he might, could not figure out anything worse than emptying his wallet for half a tank of gas. Despite the regret his ability to let it slide would most likely cause, he just had to ask-tell, "Bro, you can't mean that shit. There's no other downside."

Herb sat up straight and laid his book on the end table. "Let me think of a way to explain it, so even an idiot might understand."

Bud smiled. "And then he can tell it to me, right?"

Herb nodded, and managed a slight laugh before he continued. "Alright, see if you can follow. First of all, reliable sources caution that the world's known oil reserves aren't enough to last even another fifty years."

Bud shook his head, "No way, bro!"

"It's a fact," Herb said. "If we add that supply shortage to an ever-rising demand from developing nations, that timespan will only decrease. As we move forward in time and supplies dwindle toward zero, crude prices are guaranteed to skyrocket. Plus, when you throw in all the associated environmental danger – air pollution and $CO_2$, oil spills, toxic wastes, and damages caused by drilling – a strong case can be made that higher fuel costs are actually better for the planet."

Seeing as he truly did not give a shit, Bud only semi paid attention, with the hope that Herb would eventually run out of lecture gas and then they'd be able to figure out some lunch plans.

"Blah, blah, blah…" Herb droned on like an overplayed minor radio hit – annoying, but not so awful that it's worth getting off the couch to shut that shit off.

Herb barked, "Are you listening, fucker?"

"Sure, dude. This shit's almost interesting."

"Okay then," Herb said. "Another huge negative factor: the U.S. economy is dangerously dependent on a resource controlled by the oil-producing nations of OPEC."

Bud's bong-hit-prep stopped on a dime. "Wait, I thought OPEC was an oil company?"

Herb shook his head. "No, it is a cartel – a monopoly of nations that unapologetically circumvents markets by fixing prices. They despise us, even though they gain all of their wealth and power from American's love of gas-guzzling V8s and our insatiable addiction to crude oil."

"I love the internal combustion engine," Bud said. He began mumbling numbers as he counted on his fingers. "There's got to be... wait, let me make sure." Another quick, mumbling finger tally and then he said, "There's got to be billions and billions of them. I bet even if some brainiac actually invented a better technology – tomorrow morning – it would take decades of round-the-clock work to replace that many engines."

"It would be worth every sacrifice and cost." Herb let out a mighty sigh. "But I'm not optimistic things will change any time soon. There are far too many vested interests getting fat off the destruction of this planet, and they've proven more than willing to use every dirty trick in the book to keep the status quo."

"I bet it's all a total load of crap." Bud raised his volume to the upper limits of friendly disagreement. "Fifty years' worth of oil, my ass. You're making that shit up, or some book you read is making it up. That number has to be a worst-case, meteor-hitting-earth scenario."

"I wish that I was." Herb showed his friend the hand. "Will you please let me finish?"

Bud motored right on through the stop sign. "Why doesn't our government make money from our oil like OPEC does?" His hand clenched into a fist as he offered his simple solution. "We could form a cartel and kick that cartel's ass."

"It is what it is, my friend," Herb said. "But as I was saying…"

"Not so fast, fucker," Bud said. "How are people gonna fuckin' drive? If what you say is true, why doesn't everybody fuckin' know about it?"

An exasperated Herb stared with a very familiar shut-the-fuck-up look. "Are you ever going to let me finish explaining, dude?"

Having made his fucking point, Bud nodded, put on his second-best pretend to listen face, and set forth loading another bowl.

Pseudo-professor Herb continued lecturing, "For the sake of argument, assume that I am correct; there is only a fifty-year supply of oil. Can you please accept that for the few short minutes that it will take for me to finish?"

Bud's head nodded in time with the song playing between his ears, which Herb interpreted as a green light. "My guess is that when only a decade, or even less, of the world's oil reserves remain, the government and their corporate overlords will be forced into publicly acknowledging the dire truth. The good news is, not everyone is sitting around with their thumbs up their asses waiting for Armageddon. As we speak, numerous scientists and entrepreneurs are feverishly researching new technologies to address this very issue. They understand that to be secure as a nation, we must concentrate all our efforts on the development of renewable, alternative fuel technology."

Bud blew smoke in his face. "Alternative fuel – is that like alternative music?"

Herb grimaced. "Yeah, it's kind of like that – only different, fucker!"

Smiling, Bud shrugged. "Man, things are way better now. Remember all that thick-ass smog choking the skies when we were little kids? Today's engine technology already helps the environment. Look around, we got way more cars clogging up the fuckin' roads, and at the same time literally tons less smog than twenty years ago."

"All that you speak of is hundred-year-old technology," Herb said. "We need twenty-first-century technological solutions to eradicate the filthy gasoline engine. We have twenty-first-century light bulbs, so why not twenty-first-century transportation?"

Bud nodded while exhaling a thunderhead worth of mind-altering smoke and watched hypnotically while orphaned wisps drifted from the bong's mouthpiece.

A few minutes later, Bud's trance came to an abrupt conclusion when he sat up straight and with a huge grin said, "I just came up with the best idea ever, bro."

Herb smiled like a giant LED light bulb lit up over his head. "Me too," he said with glassy-eyed gaze fixed forward toward some faraway place where only lunatics and dreamers dare venture. "Are you thinking what I'm thinking?"

"That depends on what you're thinking," Bud said. "I'm thinking we should hit the titty bar and grab some pizza and wings."

"As usual, we are on different pages," Herb said. "Actually, we're in totally different books, dude. What I was thinking is,

'Why wait for someone else to develop the next-generation fuel?'"

Bud raised an eyebrow. "Because, we're lazy stoners?"

"Speak for yourself, dickhead. I am going to design and build an alternatively fueled vehicle." Herb bounced around in his seat like a toddler on grandpa's knee. "This is right up my alley, and exactly the kind of project I envisioned when I bought this place. Must I always remind you, the Chinese symbol for crisis is also the symbol of opportunity? This crisis presents us with an opportunity to better our world."

Like the slow kid from school that he often partied with at the back of the special bus, Bud awkwardly loaded a bowl while grumbling, "Dude, changing the world sure sounds like a whole bunch of work. Do you even know what kind of alternative fuel?"

Herb sat silently, thinking-wheels churning and grinding between his ears. A moment later, he shrugged. "I don't know... Yet! But I guarantee you that after a little brainstorming I will come up with a plan."

Bud offered his friend the freshly loaded bong. "Whatever the question is, four out of five stoners surveyed agree – weed's the answer. So, here you go. Brainstorm away, bro!"

"That's a fantastic idea!" Herb grinned, devoured the bowl with a mighty puff 'n' huff, and then sprang to his feet. "Call Frank, tell him to come over right away. We have a new project to start."

"I'd rather stay a lazy stoner," groaned Bud.

"Your parents must be so proud," Herb said. "Think they played bongos on your soft spot when you were an infant?"

Bud laughed. "I don't think so. They're not very musical."

"Besides, dude – hard work made this country great," Herb said.

Bud disagreed with a shake of his head, snickered, and then pumped his fist. "Hard work, guns, and whiskey made our country great, bro!"

"Guns are destroying America," Herb said. "They should be banned."

"You've never been more wrong in your life. Guns keep free people free."

Herb stared coldly for a quick second, but gave up with a shrug. "Whatever, man. There's no time to explain it to you right now. I'll be in my workshop. Call me the second Frank gets here."

Frank arrived two hours later. In an instant, his butt was deepening its impression in its preferred spot of the couch. Right smack dab in the middle of his landing, Frank said, "Light it up, buddy."

"Right on, bro." Bud fetched a joint from the wooden stash box on the corner table. With a dopey smirk, he passed the doobie from the left-hand side. "You do the honors."

A few hits later, Frank sunk down even further into the sofa cushions and then looked around. "Where's Herb?"

"He's in the workshop," Bud said. "I'll call him." He punched some numbers into the phone, and two seconds later blurted, "Frank's here," into the receiver faster than an auctioneer in a room full of spastics and then hung up without waiting for a reply.

"What does Herb need me for?" Frank asked.

"I'm not really sure," Bud said. "I did that bomb Canada bit you told me. Herb fuckin' hated it, gave me a fuckin' half-hour lecture. Then he told me to get you over here."

"Guess you're right about him taking everything way too serious lately," Frank said.

"Told ya, man." Bud threw up his arms while huffing and puffing. "The worst part of it is, now he's dreamed up some dumb-ass scheme and wants to bust our asses working on it. I, for one, am gonna tell him to fuck off."

Frank gave a wink and a nod. "I'll just tell him I'm all booked up."

A few moments later, Herb shuffled in, carrying himself like a hungover Eeyore heading to Pooh's funeral, far removed from the almost cheery person that left for his workshop only a few hours before. He did perk up a bit when he saw Frank. "Hey, dude, thanks for coming."

Frank returned the fist bump with far more zeal than the lethargic one sent his way. "No problem, man. When Bud said you needed me, I finished what I was doing, drove her to work, and headed over posthaste. What's up, bro?"

Herb took a deep breath. As he slowly exhaled, an almost happy smile began to form but faded away quick. "You guys remember yesterday, when we talked about my talents and education being wasted?"

"Bro, you got to quit whining about how life plays out." Frank assured him, "Everything is exactly as it is supposed to be."

Even though he stood mere inches from the guys, Herb was someplace far away. He spoke slow and soft, like a stranger at your door explaining how they just ran over your cutest, most cuddly kitty. "I mean, well, you know, me wasting my life away. I've always believed that we are all on this earth for a reason. And I've spent the better part of three decades doing absolutely worthless crap – without achieving anything significant – squandering away the years, polluting my mind with weed."

Bud blurted out, "What about the Weeble Bong? You invented that." He sang with the gusto of a piss-drunk choir boy, "Weeble Bong wobbles, but it won't fall down, la la la la la." He laughed giddily and scratched his belly, but not at the same time.

The Weeble Bong was an invention that Herb perfected a few years earlier. Basically a spill-proof bong. When Bud noticed that the bong looked like the Weeble toys he played with as a small child, he talked Herb into the name, which wasn't that hard. The legal, design, tooling, and manufacturing expenses almost bankrupted Herb.

"Yeah, Bud's right, that was a brilliant idea destined to make the world an even happier place for clumsy stoners throughout the land." Frank shook his head. "If it wasn't for those uptight pricks at Hasbro and their overzealous legal team, you'd have made millions off that bong."

"I know, I know, but I'm done with all that," Herb said. "That was a pipe dream, not a real accomplishment. I'm talking about doing something that really matters – really matters!"

Frank chuckled a bit. "'Pipe dream.' That's pretty funny, dude!"

"Fuck all that bullshit." Herb groaned and stomped his foot. "I'm trying to make a point. I've had it with the 'Evil Weed' ruling my brain and stealing my dreams."

"There you go, bagging on bud again," Frank said.

Bud scratched his head. "You're bagging on me, bro?"

"I was talking about marijuana, dumbass!" Herb pleaded, "Will you idiots please let me finish?"

Frank and Bud sat there all ears and elbows, like seals jonesing for mackerel, waiting for the money shot.

"I have decided, and really mean it this time – I refuse to let cannabis bring me down any longer," Herb said. "I will use weed to get me high in a whole different way. But I will need lots of help and support from both of you." He pumped his fist. "Will you guys help me change the world for the better?"

"Not a chance." Bud stood up. "Let's order some Thai food."

"Hold on a second. I want to hear this," Frank said. "What's your plan, dude?"

"Well, I am going to design and build an alternatively fueled vehicle," Herb said.

With a slight tilt of his head, Frank asked, "What kind of fuel, Herb?"

"Yes," said Herb.

While waiting for further explanation, Frank looked more baffled than a cross-eyed puppy gazing into a funhouse mirror. Bud looked brain-dead, as victims of public schools often do.

Frank gave it another try. "What is your energy source going to be, Herb?"

"Yes it is!" Herb grinned and then attempted to let the wordplay marinate, but couldn't hold back even a second longer. The words tumbled from his mouth so fast that they sounded absurd, as though he said, "We, my friends, are going to make a car run on weed!"

In a flash of realization, a wide grin spread across Frank's face. "Yeeeeeeeeeeeeee-fucking-haaaaaaaaaaaaaaaw," he walloped. "That'll be an honest-to-goodness green-powered ride. Best part is, if the car gets an exhaust leak, there's no need to fix it."

Bud tilted his head a little bit sideways and then slowly nodded as he too joined in on the smile party. "That actually sounds like a fun project. How many miles to the ounce do you think she'll get?"

Herb, caught off guard by an overwhelming positive reaction and lack of pushback, paused for a moment to ponder. "Interesting question," he said. "We won't know how many MPOZ until we have a prototype up and running."

"Awesome," said Frank. "When do you plan on starting?"

"Crack of noon tomorrow," Herb said. "That is, if you guys are down."

Frank gestured in Bud's direction. "I'm good to go if he's down for it."

"Actually, I'm totally into that shit," Bud said. "How about barbecue instead of Thai?"

# 3

Eleven thirty the next morning, Bud and Herb were kicking it at the dining table awaiting Frank's arrival.

As always, Bud got a good night's rest, but a marijuana crop doesn't tend itself. So most mornings, soon after the rooster crowed, he was up attending to the enterprise's horticultural necessities.

After Herb made him "get rid of that fucking rooster," Bud bought an alarm clock.

Herb had pulled an all-nighter, only managing to pry himself from his work early in the a.m. to catch a power nap and then be up in time to explain his latest plan to the guys. Despite the grind and lack of sleep, the excitement of a new project had him super energized like a five-year-old after slamming three espressos.

While Herb engaged in jumbled stream of confusing idea explaining, Bud tuned it all out and busied himself rolling up a half-ounce worth of joints meant to last throughout the day, depending on if any wheels needed greasing along his coming foray into the outside world.

"Hey, bro, I just thought of something," Bud said. "Don't we have to get a car before we can begin the project?"

"I'm way ahead of you, dude," Herb said. "While you were busy destroying brain cells the second you woke up, I sent Frank to acquire a cheap rolling canvas for my project."

Bud snapped like an angry dog being tormented by an espresso-loving five-year-old. "Bro, it wasn't so long ago that you'd have a few bongloads before setting out to face the cruel world. So do me a fuckin' favor, quit the holier-than-thou shit!"

Pointing out facts at high volume got Herb hot under the collar. "Dude, for your information, I have never smoked pot before even taking a leak in the morning."

Bud grinned like a wolf shedding sheep's clothing. "That's not true; me and Frank shotgunned you massive hits a million times while you were asleep."

Herb's brow furrowed, "Really?"

Bud grinned and lied, "Nope, just kidding."

Frank and Bud had not actually shotgunned Herb anywhere near a million times, but as of late those two did it quite often. The un-wake n' bake pot party started out as a whim-prank, but they soon realized that every time Herb woke up stoned, he was in a splendid mood and often cooked up a spectacular breakfast feast for everyone.

One morning's bountiful stacks of scrumptious chopped apple pecan pancakes, griddled to golden perfection then topped with heaps of melting butter and pure maple syrup, convinced Bud that he needed something to take the work out of shotgunning a tossing and turning moving target so that he could forever skip Denny's Bland Scams.

It only took Bud half a day to engineer a serviceable device made up of a fish tank pump connected to thirty feet of rubber tubing, a nozzle, and a few fittings. The finished product, which he deemed the "BurnRiteReeferInjector," pumped smoke from a joint with the flick of a switch and sent it flowing out the other end of the tube's nozzle until the joint was no more. It was top secret, so he hid it in the tool room because Herb never went in there.

Frank arrived just in the nick of time to distract Herb from any follow-up questions about passive sleep smoking. He crossed the kickback room toward the kitchenette, carrying two medium-sized brown paper bags. "Hey, dudes, I grabbed a grip of apple fritters and some chocolate milk."

Bud lunged straight for the greasier of the two bags and proclaimed, "'Breakfast of Champions.'"

"Championship bong teams, maybe." Frank laughed.

"Ha ha," Herb grouched. "Is life always a comedy skit for you two stooges?"

Frank gave a friendly shove. "Just keep in mind that there were 'Three Stooges.' Making you Moe, who was only funny because he was such a dick."

"Yeah-yeah." Herb managed a slight laugh. "Fuck you, Frank. What's up with getting me a car?"

"I scored a Dodge Caravan for next to nothing," Frank motioned toward the front door. "Dummy should have held out for a full ounce."

"Awesome, man. This is all coming together beautifully." Herb patted him on the back. "That means you two can start taking measurements and make me an initial checklist first thing tomorrow morning."

Sporting a chocolate-milk mustache, Bud finished grinding the last bite of fritter then washed it down by lighting a fat joint. "That's perfect. Let's celebrate!"

With almost a quarter of the doobie puffed up in smoke, Frank tired of waiting for the pass and wrestled it away, sucked up an immense toke, and then coughed and hacked like a TB victim from nineteenth-century London. Red-faced with watery eyes, he eked out, "I didn't get a hit."

Bud had a hearty laugh while Herb scowled.

Frank took another puff, passed it back, poured a cup of chocolate milk, and grabbed a fritter.

Bud stood and brushed a few crumbs from his pants. "I'm gonna cut out of here."

Herb grimaced and pointed to the floor. "No wonder we have ants. Vacuum that shit up."

"I'm telling ya, if we had a puppy, he'd be on those crumbs." Bud took a hefty toke.

"For the hundredth time, no way." Herb grumbled and swatted away the incoming joint. "It's too early for weed. Plus, we have too much work to get done. Where are you going, anyway? If it isn't life or death, stay here."

Bud shrugged it off. "I gotta pick up a washer and dryer that my buddy don't want no more, before someone else beats me to it."

Bud began vacuuming a spot about four feet from where he should have, while Herb yelled above the hand vac's irritating whine, "You always get sidetracked by the stupidest shit!"

Bud switched the vacuum off and nodded. "You know what they say, 'One man's sidetrack is another man's wife.'"

"No one ever says that," Herb grumbled and snatched the vacuum away to take matters into his own hands.

Frank leisurely exhaled a few cubic yards of smoke. "Does that mean we're done for today?"

Herb dumped four crumbs into the trashcan and clicked the vac back into the recharger. "No, I need you to head downtown to check for existing patents."

"Based on what?" said Frank.

"Last night I sketched out a basic design, and made a list of possible paths toward accomplishing my goal." Herb waved an arm toward his drafting table. "Come check out my preliminary ideas. That should give you a better idea of what to look for."

Frank examined the sketch for a few minutes. "You really think that'll work?"

Herb shrugged, and maybe almost smiled. It was hard to tell – could have been gas. "We won't know until we try. It's a pretty basic principle, quite similar to the way a diesel electric train operates. I plan on using energy derived from marijuana plant mass instead of diesel oil to fuel a mini power plant that generates on-demand electricity."

Frank reviewed the designs once again. "You gonna use weed oil?"

Herb shook his head. "Probably not. My goal is for an ultra-clean, non-combustion energy conversion. There are several ways of harnessing potential energy locked in plant matter. My task is figuring out which is the most efficient method using marijuana's biomass. I need you to research if anyone holds patents like this drawing."

Frank nodded and smiled. "No problem, man."

"I made you a copy and a list of terms to help your search." Herb pointed to a tube leaning by the lobby door. "Right over there."

"And if no one has, you need me to grab the proper paperwork for you to stake your claim?" asked Frank.

"Exactly," said Herb.

Wearing a dopey grin, Bud joined them. "We should develop a strain of O.G. Diesel. That way the Caravan will run on weed and diesel, too."

Frank deadpanned, "Don't quit your day job, bro."

As Bud's smile widened, a bit of drool tried escaping from the side of his mouth, but he caught it with his sleeve. "I don't have a day job, so please laugh at my jokes."

"You do have a day job, moron," Herb barked. "For the foreseeable future, you have major responsibilities."

Bud pondered for a flash then raised his hand.

Herb gave him an angry stare. "Yes, Bud?"

"Doing what?"

Herb went from simmer to boil. "You smoke way too much pot, dude. I shouldn't have to remind you that tomorrow we will begin building a revolutionary concept vehicle, and that it will require you to work your 'lazy stoner' ass off."

Bud shrugged. "Man, bottom line – it's just a car. You get the parts and tell us what you want, and then Frank and me will slap that shit together in no time flat. It's all on you, brother. So handle your business and I'll handle mine. Try smoking some pot to chill the fuck out, you uptight prick."

"That's your solution for everything," Herb screeched. "I cannot believe you are about to drive after smoking that much pot."

"I'm less agro when I drive stoned, so I never do shit that pisses people off," Bud said.

Frank laughed. "Yeah, right. What about the poor schlep stuck behind your three-horse-power VW Bus inching its way up a steep grade? Talk about pissing people off."

Bud nodded. "True, but either way, I'm out of here."

Frank punched him in the arm. "Later, dude."

"Make sure you just get those appliances and come straight back here," Herb said. "I need your help later."

Bud replied with a noncommittal wave.

As the door shut behind Bud, Herb's jaw muscles unclenched enough that he was able to smile longer than a flash.

He put a hand on Frank's shoulder. "I just had a great idea. While you're at it, check to see if I can get some kind of government grant funding. I can knock out a research proposal in a week."

With a sly smile, Frank slapped him on the back. "Great idea, and if anyone asks what kind of alternative fuel, I'll just tell them it's an easily-cultivated, high-output biomass fuel. 'Ask not what you can do for your country, but what your country can do for you.'"

"We are doing something for the country. And our planet," Herb said. "But research assistance is always helpful and appreciated." He raised it up for a high five. "This is all coming together great."

Frank hit him back with a high hand slap. "Guess I better get going and be done with it. I need to rest up for a few hot dates tonight."

"I'll be in my lab searching through online journals, boning up on the state of any similar research," Herb said. "Talk to you later, man."

Frank grabbed the drawing, and the door was closed almost all the way behind him when he stuck his foot in the way and yelled back through the crack, "Yo, bro, before I split, come check out the Caravan."

Herb was only a few seconds behind, but when he stepped out the front door, except for a bewildered-looking Frank, the parking lot was empty.

Frank looked about while scratching his head. "Fucking car thieves strike again," he said. "I understand Bud's Camaro getting ripped off, but who'd want a beat up Caravan?"

Herb walked all the way out to the curb and then panned his head slowly from right to left to see if the van was parked close by for some unexplained reason.

He turned to face his building and then scanned the property high and low in all directions before heading back to the front door. "I need more cameras in my parking lot, ASAP."

# 4

When it came to overdoing shit, Herb just couldn't seem to help himself. The minivan getting snatched from right under his nose left him confounded and unsettled, so he rushed right out to buy twenty grand worth of state-of-the-art gadgets and then insisted, by throwing a hissy fit, that Bud drop everything to help him with the "security upgrades."

In reality, those two undertook a complete overhaul of the existing system, spending the better part of three days installing a hard-drive controller, various sensors and alarms, sixteen computer-controlled cameras with microphones, and enough video monitors – come fall – to simultaneously watch every Sunday football game.

With work complete almost to Herb's satisfaction, Bud rewarded himself several times for a job well done and then set down the Weeble Bong. While reloading, he once again admired his handiwork through a lingering haze. "If we woulda done all this stuff last month, I'd still have my fuckin' Chevy," he grouched. "Sucks we had the whole set up watching only the inside, but anyone could take whatever they wanted from outside."

Herb waved off the incoming bong and snarled, "How many more fucking times are you going to tell me that shit?"

A buzzing alarm demanded a shift of focus to the bank of security monitors, showing Frank out front dismounting his Harley.

"Whatever, you're a dick. I'll go let him in," said Bud.

Upon their return, Herb skipped the pleasantries. "What's the word on my Dodge?"

"Still no luck on the car situation, buddy," Frank said. "It wasn't towed, and I can't report it stolen because it's not registered in my name. I told the cops that it was the second car stolen from the lot in under a month. To my absolute surprise, they didn't give a shit."

"Just like always," Herb moaned. "I feel absolutely powerless. Wish I could do something instead of just waiting around for the world to slide it in deeper."

"Indeed, some fucked up shit," Frank said. "But I'll keep to it until I get you some better answers, promise."

"Thanks, man." Herb waved an arm at the monitors. "Until we figure out who keeps stealing vehicles from out front, it's probably wise to park everything behind the fence out back."

Frank nodded. "Great idea. That's why I parked my bike in the lobby."

"What's the status about possible research funds?" Herb asked.

"I got some good news and bad news." Frank put an arm around his shoulder. "Bad news is, no dice on the government cheese for marijuana research."

Herb spun to extract himself from the personal contact and then waited for more information. When none appeared forthcoming, he said, "I thought you had some good news, too."

"Oh yeah, this super-fine chick working the counter, well, she sucked my dick on her lunch break." Frank grabbed his crotch, thrust his hips, and grinned.

"Sure she did." Herb scowled. "I'm getting sick of bullshit, so please spare me any more fictions."

Frank turned to Bud and smile-nodded, letting him know it was no joke.

Bud high fived his hero. "I just had a great idea. We could make Frank's motorcycle run on weed."

"We are building an alternative fuel car," Herb grumbled. "Motorcycles already get great mileage, but are impractical and dangerous."

"I guess you're right." Bud shrugged. "Anyways, Harleys are only good if you want to build a vehicle that runs on crank."

"Funny ha-ha, guys." Frank mock strangled Bud and, while he held a captive audience, threw in a couple noogies. "There's no frickin' way I'd ever let you tear up my dangerously exciting, yet extremely-practical-for-the-single-stud bike."

Bud chuckled as he broke free and stumbled away. "How bout we use my Bus?"

"That old piece of junk?" Herb scoffed. "No way, not for my project!" He started toward his workshop. "You know where to find me if you come up with any non-moronic suggestions."

"Wait," Frank said. "Actually, Bud's V-Dub is perfect. What could be better than a 1972 Volkswagen Bus running on weed? For decades the driver has run on weed. Now we can make the Bus run on pot power."

"Plus, it's bought and paid for and already parked ten feet away from your laboratory." Bud sold it with a fist pump.

Herb stopped in his tracks and turned back around, mumbling, "May-be… it might be kind of fitting…" Wearing a half smile, he continued with a bit more zeal. "And if we want to get started right away, I guess we really have no choice. Okay, let's do it."

Bud smiled like someone who finally won an argument after hundreds of tries. Because he just won an argument after hundreds of tries. "I thought you'd like my idea. But if we're going to use my Bus, I need her for a few days; be back in a couple of hours."

"I have a lot of things to do later," Herb hollered. "Make damn sure you're back by two so you can keep an eye on this place while I'm out."

Bud gave a dismissive wave. "With all your new high-tech security crap, this place is more secure than Fort Knox. But I'll for sure be back by two so you can help me unload that washer and dryer sitting in my Bus for days."

Bud returned just past one in the afternoon and parked in the side lot next to the rollup garage door.

Herb was not at his workbench, so Bud went to bellow down the hall toward kickback area, "Herrrrrrrrrb – Fraaaannk, you guys here?"

Crickets.

Bud grumbled, "Great, now I gotta unload this crap all by myself."

He made a quick trip to the kickback area to double-check for the guys and to make sure that the Weeble Bong was safe and operable.

On his way back out, he wedged the hall door open and continued to mumble-grumble all the way outside, "mrfen fric en grrrr lle fuckin'…"

It wasn't too long before Bud returned with an ancient washing machine, teetering on a dolly that he trucked toward the kickback room.

He paused at the end of the hall while deciding on a final location, and indulged in a bit more grumbling. "Fuckin' asshole, can't even help me once."

It didn't take long to settle on a spot along the wall separating the kickback area from the grow space, just about under the wall of video monitors. After dropping off the washer, he repeated the process with the dryer – minus the grumbling, so it went a little quicker.

Mechanically gifted, it took him less than two hours for the hook-up. It was an easy install, because of a water supply and drain right there inside the wall already being used for the grow room.

After tidying up and returning the tools, he crammed a load of stinky work Levis into the washing machine, then set the cycle in motion.

With nothing else to do, he plopped onto the couch and snapped five quick bong rips in a row. A few hundred thousand fizzled brain cells later, Bud stood and went to the drafting table, where he pondered Herb's design ideas.

After ten minutes of semi-focused gaze, with intermittent head and ball scratching, Bud said, "I guess I'll have to update this drawing a wee bit."

He reached for a pen, folded back Herb's original drawing, and got to work on a fresh sheet of paper.

Half an hour later, Bud put the finishing touches on his sketch by adding a title: "Herb's Love Bus." He set the pen down and proclaimed, "There, that ought to do it."

Bud returned to the couch so he and the Weeble could do The Monkey.

It wasn't too much later that Herb returned, took one look at Bud vegging on the couch, and, without even a hello, launched straight into him. "I thought we both agreed, so that this project gets done quickly, we wouldn't smoke pot all damn day."

"That doesn't sound like something I'd agree too," Bud said with a smile. "But, bro, I haven't smoked pot since this morning."

Herb went into full-on dad mode. "What's that smell, then?"

Bud kept a straight face while explaining, "Well, after I hooked up the washer – when I was cleaning up – the vacuum cleaner belt burned up and broke." He waved a hand in front of his nose. "Tons of stinky smoke, bro."

Herb shook his head and grumbled, "Sure you did," all the while looking more disgusted than one who happened upon their grandparents doing some extra-dirty banging.

Bud laughed, "I'm just kidding. Of course I smoked pot. The answer to that question is always yes!"

Herb must never have heard the old saying about catching more flies with honey, so he spoke with his usual vinegar. "I have told you a hundred times, and I'm getting tired of repeating myself. 'There is way too much work to do, and no time to mess around getting sidetracked!' We squandered the last decade with buds, babes, beer, and video games. Don't you ever get bored with all that high school crap? I thought you agreed that it's time to get serious."

Bud employed his favorite survival technique, which no doubt had saved him from numerous assault charges – he ignored Herb and nodded as soon as the yabbering ceased.

After Herb got most of it out of his system, he softened his tone a bit. Almost imploring, he said, "I really do need your undivided support and complete focus for this project. What do you say, brother? Are you with me?"

Bud whimpered, "I've been working all day."

"You worked on your sidetrack, not the real project," Herb said. "Are you with me or against me, dude?"

Bud's eyes widened and a giant smile spread across his face. He shouted out with glee, "Hey wait, I just remembered. I have been working on the project. Check out my drawing on the drafting table."

Herb went to look over the artwork, and it wasn't long before he smiled. He held that smile. "Wow, 'Herb's Love Bus.' Excellent concept – I love it! Your old bucket of bolts has never looked finer!"

"Thanks, bro." Bud smiled like a toddler after two shots of tequila, once the head shaking and tequila face goes away.

"One slight change." Herb picked up the marker and scribbled something on the pad. "There, 'Bud's Love Bus' is much better. No point in going to war with that Mussolini Mouse!"

"Right on," said Bud. "My love Bus lives on."

Herb pointed toward the recently installed appliances. "It sounds like that washing machine is running."

Bud nodded. "Yep, sure is. I had some jeans that were so dirty that I had to wash them twice. In about five minutes they'll…"

Interrupted by a sudden silence following the washer's completed final-spin racket, Bud sidetracked midsentence to go toss jeans into the dryer. Setting the dial for sixty minutes, he pushed start. The dryer hummed to life with clanking thuds as he turned around and smiled. "Got any dirty clothes that need some washing?"

Before Herb had a chance to answer, the buzzing alarm drew their attention to the security monitors, where two men in cheap suits, dark glasses, and matching black, rubber-soled uniform shoes snooped around the front parking lot. On the other hand, those two trespassers were far from uniform, one being a white guy around fifty years old, the other a black guy in his mid twenties.

Bud pointed and cried out, "I saw those same two dudes the day my Camaro disappeared."

With eyes glued to the monitors, Herb slowly shook his head. "Who are they? They look like cops, not car thieves."

"If they're the assholes who snatched my ride, we need to find out who the fuck they are," Bud said. "Looks like it's time to run all this new security shit through its paces."

"Yes indeed." Herb nodded and broke toward the stairs. "I'll head to the roof. You man the command center down here."

Bud agreed with the plan of action by yelling, "Right on!"

Herb made the briefest of detours to retrieve his commando gear, parabolic microphone, and two-way radio.

Moments later, Herb settled into a position on the roof where he could direct action from the best tactical view. He who owns the high ground owns the battlefield. Peering through his field glasses from beneath a camouflage tarp, he tracked the men as they made their way to the street corner. They paused for a moment before rounding the corner to travel farther along the sidewalk running parallel to the warehouse.

Inside, Bud camped out just below the wall of video screens, a fat joint dangling from his lips and his laptop resting on his knees, while he puffed and clicked away on the keyboard controlling the whole shebang. Except for a few blind and dead spots, he enjoyed real-time audio-visual surveillance of just about every square inch of the building's perimeter. As he followed the men from camera to camera and screen to screen, a hard drive captured every sight and sound.

From his scout's nest high above, Herb tracked the unknown strangers strolling along as if they didn't have a care in the world. The prey stopped just past the side parking lot's gate, in one of the camera's blind spots.

Bud had shifted attention to finding a lighter, but upon refocusing to the task at hand could not relocate the mystery men on any video screen. He radioed, "I've lost visual. You see where they went, right on?"

"I have eyes on them," Herb reported. "Target is stationary on the sidewalk, approximately twenty feet from northwest perimeter, over."

"They're out of sound range, too?" Bud asked. "Can you get audio on these guys, right on?"

Herb aimed his parabolic microphone at the men and then radioed back, "If they talk, I'll get them. I'm patching you the audio feed, make sure to get it on the hard drive, over."

The younger and far darker-complexioned of the two suit-wearing prowlers said, "Let's get out of here."

While facing three quarters away from the warehouse, with head turned ever so slightly to observe the building from the corner of an eye, the man did not respond. Instead, he made a big production of retrieving a phone from his pocket, to answer a phone that did not ring.

"Come on, Thursday," said the second man. "Let's go."

Thursday spoke into the receiver, "Just a minute, Agent Jefferson."

Jefferson did not seem to care enough to play along with the stealth-mode bullshit. He stood at the ready in an almost boxers' stance, facing the building, glaring straight across the parking lot toward the rollup door. "We really need to go and take care of other cases, partner. There's nothing to see here."

Thursday disregarded the suggestion and began inching back toward the warehouse. "Looks like there's no one around. Let's see if we can get in that gate."

Jefferson remained cautious as he followed, stopping a few feet short of his partner to assess the obstacle before them. "It's locked," he said. "I don't like this at all."

Herb radioed, "Targets are heading our way, over."

"I got 'em," Bud said. "Did I hear that fuck-wad say he's gonna break in, right on?"

Herb barked, "Shush up, fucker, over."

Thursday said, "I want to dig up some dirt to strengthen our case."

"What are you talking about?" Jefferson grumbled while kicking at the ground. "We shouldn't have even come back here."

Mere inches from the side parking lot's gate, Thursday turned to fully face the building and take in the property's layout. "Hey, partner, just come over here for a second. Warn me if you see anyone coming."

Jefferson crept closer. "I don't see the point in all this snooping."

"Let's hop over real quick and do a little recon," suggested Thursday.

"You're on your own," Jefferson said. "I'm not going in there."

Herb sounded the alert, "That asshole is actually going to scale my fence. Stand by for my signal to commence 'Operation Eye-Opener,' over!"

"Awesome possum," said Bud. "On your signal, it's a go for 'Eye-Opener,' right on."

The instant that Thursday placed his second hand onto the fence, Herb barked, "Go-go-go, light up this guy, over!"

Like a way-too-stoned Mozart performing acid-electronica, Bud punched Ctrl+Shift+Z simultaneously on his keyboard, triggering a remote switch that unleashed 200,000 volts into the metal fence and then straight through Thursday's hands and on out through the soles of his feet in search of the nearest ground. Lucky for him, the shock was low amperage. Because volts don't kill, amps do.

Thursday didn't appear to feel so lucky – he convulsed and shook like an epileptic on a vibrating bed during an earthquake and sang something like, "Arrrggg-hhhh-ahhhhhh-fuuuuuuuarrrrrrrrrrrga-ga-guh-guh," channeled directly up from the pit of his soul. Strangely enough, it sounded very similar to a not-so-popular-song from the early eighties.

Inside, Bud experienced a few minor issues of his own. The instant that he activated the switch to power up the fence, the monitor screens flickered and then sparks began showering down from behind them. Before the overhead lights went dark, he noticed steam rising from behind the dryer, making an insidious climb to the video screens and the security system's hard-drive controller.

Bud almost jumped out of his shoes, caught the laptop before it hit the floor, and then tossed it aside to dive toward the dryer and yank open the door to stop the steam.

Bud's predicament inside meant that outside not even a full second passed before the shocking ended, which froze Thursday in place before he could perform a second verse.

Disappointed with Bud's lack of punitive aggression, Herb groaned over the radio, "Aw, dude, you should have lit that fucker up for at least ten seconds, over."

Swallowed by pitch-black, and unwilling to give an accurate report of his current situation, Bud said, "The computer began rebooting on its own right when I triggered 'Eye-Opener.' Should be all good in thirty seconds, right on."

By the flickering flame of the lighter burning his thumb, Bud yanked plugs from receptacles and then, with thumb tip in mouth, inched his way along the wall, feeling for the circuit-breaker box.

Meanwhile, outside, Jefferson grabbed Thursday by his belt to yank him from the fence, spun him around, then waltzed him away and eased him down to a seat on the curb.

Herb followed their movements from high above. "Can you see target, over?"

No reply.

"Bud, do you read me? Come in," Herb begged. "I have target in sight, stationary between two parked cars. Will advise if they come your way, over."

To Bud's delight, the lights came on the instant the main breaker got reset. He raced back to his walkie-talkie and paused for a heartbeat to catch his breath before clicking the transmit button. "Okay, bro, you keep an eye on them and let me know if they try to breech again, right on."

"Roger that, over," Herb said.

Bud's wishful thinking meant that all the gear was no worse for wear or tear. All he needed to do was dry it off and reboot the system; easy-peasy. To that end, he wiped down the wall and began dabbing wiring with paper towels.

A giant mound of wadded paper formed at his feet, but there seemed to be little or no progress in moisture removal from the equipment's nooks and crannies. Bud scurried to retrieve a second roll of towels. Halfway back, he screeched to a halt. "Oh, fuck yeah, that's it!"

Bud made double time retrieving a hair dryer and then got to blow drying.

Back outside on the street, five minutes after his electrifying performance, Thursday took a heave of breath, stood almost straight up, brushed himself off, wiped some sweat from the back of his neck, ran fingers through his hair, used a sleeve to dab a bit of moisture from the corners of his mouth, and topped it all off with a wave of the middle finger at the building. "Forget about these assholes. Let's get the hell out of here!"

"It's about time," Jefferson said. "We should have just gone to the front door and settled this shit once and for all."

The two agents set off toward the street that fronted Herb's warehouse, with Thursday charging straight ahead like a bronco with blinders, but Jefferson's head seemed on a swivel. Even the slightest shadow shift from the warehouse's direction halted him in his tracks.

"We'll see who gets the last laugh," Thursday grumbled. "Let's go to the Spy Shop and pick up some counter-surveillance gear. Next time, we will have a tactical and technological advantage over these scoundrels."

Jefferson hurried to catch up. "Yeah, sure – next time, ha!"

Upon arrival at the street corner, Thursday nudged Jefferson and motioned toward an LAPD patrol car parked up the block.

They made a beeline for the cop.

Herb noticed the squad car for the first time when the agents changed course. To his shock and dismay, the sergeant at the wheel had field glasses trained on the front door of the warehouse.

Herb sounded the alarm, "Dude, nine-one-one, come in! We got L-E watching the nest. I repeat, LAPD squad car observing our location. You back online yet, over?"

Bud radioed back, "She'll be ready in a flash, right on."

Not much louder than a whisper, Herb begged, "Please, I need you to get that shit going ASAP, over."

"Almost there, right on," Bud said.

To alleviate his fear that the system wasn't ready to go, Bud relit the doobie and crossed his fingers before plugging in components.

Restarting the system restarted problems. Seconds into the reboot, smoke began wafting from the computer controller and the monitors took turns glowing bright blue screens before one by one going dark amongst a spectacular shower of sparks. Bud's tripping out on the light show meant that he neglected to pull any plugs until four of the monitors were reduced to blank screens, throwing off the smoldering solder stink of electrical failure.

While Bud's hopes came crashing to earth one brilliant flare at a time, Herb tracked Thursday and Jefferson making their way to the patrol car.

When they walked up on the cop, Thursday greeted him. "Hi-ya, Stan. It's been a long time, friend."

The cop dropped the binoculars and reached for his sidearm. Then a considerable smile appeared just below his push-broom of a mustache as he let the hand fall from his Glock and removed his forearm's awkward attempt of hiding the binoculars. "Well, I'll be damned. What are you doing in my neck of the woods, Thursday, old pal?"

"We came out here following up on a case." Thursday pointed to the warehouse's front door. "There are a couple low-life losers operating out of that building."

Sergeant Stan sat straight up and checked the line of sight with his thumb, just to make sure. "You know those guys? That's damn good news, I've been after those monsters ever since Lilly went to a party at that place. Did you find any probable?"

"I believe we have some information that you will find most helpful," Thursday said. "I've been watching those scumbags ever since…"

The Sergeant placed an index finger to his lips and gave a slight nod toward the roofline, "Let's go talk about this somewhere else; never can be too careful."

Jefferson spun on his heels and looked straight to where Herb was camped out.

Herb crouched down further to radio, "Bud, come in, come in. I've been made. You get the cameras up yet, over?"

Bud switched off the hair dryer. "Gimme five, we should be good. Use your super-snooper microphone while you keep an eye on them, right on."

"They're driving away, damn it," Herb barked. "I'll be right down, over and out."

"Check that," Bud said. "You should stay put, just in case they come back. Just gimme a minute and everything will be a go, right on."

Herb descended the steps three at a time and burst into the kickback area loaded for Bud-bear. When he saw the inoperable monitors, and the mess of wadded-up paper towels, and Bud blow drying the hard drive and cluster of tangled wires, he exploded like a rocket ship crashing into a supernova and began bellowing louder than usual, "Dude, what the fuck happened?"

Despite being startled, Bud remained calm, cool, and collected as he waved his arm over the discombobulated electronics like a magician ready to make a semi-attractive assistant disappear. "Oh, this? It's nothing huge. Just a little steam; I'll have it up and running in a jiffy, bro."

Herb was so furious he forgot to keep yelling. Instead, he merely asked, "Where the fuck did steam come…"

He figured out the answer on his own and spun toward the dryer. It didn't take him very long to remember to yell. "You're a total fucking moron!"

Bud shrugged. "Sorry, man. Accidents happen."

Herb went over and peeked behind the dryer. He remained facing the wall, mumbling, "What kind of imbecile decides to hook up a dryer, places wet clothes in it, and then operates that dryer in an enclosed space?"

He turned to complete the quizzing with arms waving about like an orangutan at a rave and screeched, "Next to thousands of dollars' worth of my electronics – without a fucking vent hose?"

Bud looked down at his shoelaces. "I forgot," he muttered. "Besides, it would be tough to vent from there; I'll just install one of those indoor kits and build an enclosure so that shit can't happen ag…"

"No 'indoor kit!'" Herb yelled. "Vent that shit! You always forget important shit, because you are stoned every fucking minute of every fucking day!"

Bud set down the doobie he was fixing to relight. "That's not true."

"Dude, you got a mini-bong on your night stand," said Herb.

"Look, bro, I'm sorry," Bud said. "It was an accident. I promise I'll fix it first thing tomorrow."

"You better, before you do any more fucking laundry, idiot!"

"No shit, Sherlock!" Bud pleaded. "It's over. Let's drop it before you blow an ass-artery, bitch."

"Fuck you!" Herb commanded. "Get your ass to the hardware store first thing tomorrow morning and buy whatever you need to vent that fucking dryer correctly."

"Yeah, okay," Bud grumbled. "But just remember, that electric fence was your idea. And it triggered all this destruction."

Herb did not acknowledge that tidbit of information. Nevertheless, he decreased his volume and changed the subject. "I hope we got that shit on tape. I need to listen again to hear if I missed anything."

Bud told him a pleasant and reassuring half-truth. "Yep, I got everything on the hard drive right up to the blackout."

"Good," Herb said. "Reboot the computer and let's check it out."

Bud picked up the hair dryer. "Let me just make sure everything's dry before I fire her up. Wouldn't want to cause any more damage, bro."

Herb's eyebrow arched, "'Any more damage?'"

"Yeah, we're gonna need a few replacement parts to get this rig up and running at full capacity," Bud said. "I'll make you a list."

"Guess that means we can't leave this place unattended until we get the surveillance system fixed," Herb said. "Looks like you're stuck here for the rest of the day when you get back tomorrow."

Bud stomped his foot like a teething two-year-old and whined, "Why can't you watch the fuckin' place?"

Herb remained calm. "I need to get stuff to fix the security system and for the Love Bus project. Once you get that equipment dried out, troubleshoot it and make me that parts list. We need to get it working again before those cops come back."

"Right on," Bud said. "But why do you think they're cops?"

Herb said, "You heard him say, 'Agent Jefferson,' right?"

Bud shrugged. "They could be travel agents."

Herb laughed. "Damn, dude, you're such an idiot. One thing is for sure, Sergeant Stan is definitely a cop; and he was watching this building with binoculars. Do you know a Lilly?"

"That's some high school chick who's stalking Frank." Bud chuckled. "Why, did she come by?"

"Fucking Frank," Herb said. "That cop must be her dad."

"I guarantee you that Frank didn't do nothing with her," said Bud.

"How can you possibly be sure of that?" Herb asked.

"Because I was his wing-man, so Frank could get her mother alone." Bud grinned. "And I barely smoked any pot at all with Lilly. She's a total lightweight, bro."

Herb shook his head. "Great, we're in double-deep doo-doo!"

# 5

Herb bitched and moaned and moaned and bitched on and on throughout the night, while they tried and tried and failed to recover the hard drives' jealously guarded secrets. The dead drive told no tales, because that shit was totally smoked; not unlike an ounce of weed owned by Bud the week before.

Early the next morning, before Herb's bitching and moaning started for the day, Bud set off for the hardware store. When he pulled back into the side lot, there stood Herb by the rollup garage door, arms crossed and toe tapping, glaring in beady-eyed glory through the windshield at Bud.

A cheery Bud sprang from his VW Bus and got right to unloading. "Bro, last night while I was trying to sleep, I got the best idea about what to do with the steam."

Herb growled, "Yeah, you hook that motherfucker to a vent hose, and then run it the fuck outside, asshole."

Bud's smile fell from his face. "Calm down, bro," he pleaded. "If you'd just listen for once, I got an awesome idea you're gonna love. It's real scientific, too. I saw it on Mr. Wizard when I was a kid. Plus, not only will I enclose them,

I'm gonna build a kick-ass laundry area with shelves and a countertop for folding clothes."

"I'm not interested in anything other than an old-school dryer vent hose," Herb barked. "Have that shit hooked up correctly by the time I get back, or get those fucking appliances out of my warehouse."

"My idea isn't wrong – it's just different," Bud said.

"Your different ideas often get dangerous," Herb sneered. "You know why? It's because you're a brain-dead wastoid idiot." He shook the parts list in Bud's face. "You did at least five thousand dollars in damage yesterday."

Bud swatted the paper away. "You mean 'we,' right?"

"There's only one idiot in this parking lot," Herb said. "And I'm looking straight at him."

Bud turned to look behind, to see who Herb was talking about. Once he figured it out, Bud got his sulk on and went to work offloading the lumber, sheetrock, paint, and bags of supplies.

Herb peered silently until the last bag was removed and then climbed behind the wheel and drove off.

As Herb puttered away, Bud flipped him off, but saw him watching from the mirror and shifted the gesture to a peace sign.

Bud got busy lugging supplies inside, muttering to himself, "He has no fuckin' idea what a hassle it is to run a vent hose from that location. He'd know that shit if he actually built something in real life, instead of just on his fuckin' computer."

All materials loaded inside, Bud took measurements, jotted a few notes, and then scribbled a diagram. With mindless tugging of an earlobe, he looked over the plans and thought out loud, "Maybe if I put the… Nah, fuck. That shit will never fly."

Bud went to the kitchen and made himself a sandwich. He chewed slowly while gazing across the counter toward the dryer. All of a sudden, his eyes widened like a giant slobbering cartoon cat getting outsmarted by a tiny yellow bird.

He set the hoagie down, but his excitement dissipated before he could even swallow the current bite. He grabbed his grub from the plate. "Nah, that's fucked, too."

Some ten minutes later, and still at a complete loss, he went for the couch. He just about stood up a few times, but apparently felt setting the bong down would be premature.

More frustrated than an armless teen boy picturing his friend's hot mother naked, Bud stood and bellyached, "There's no fuckin' way I can route it to the roof without going through the middle of my room. I bet he'd love it if I ran this fuckin' vent straight through the middle of his room."

His arms flung about as if he were attempting to take flight. "Can't send that shit into the grow area, either. Fuck Herb! I'm gonna do this shit my way. That dick will never be the wiser."

Bud got started by arranging all the supplies into alphabetical order. After a few trips to the shop for tools, he started pounding that shit out.

It wasn't too long before Frank showed up, offering to help out in trade for the smoking of a fatty.

As the work began in earnest, Bud filled him in on the prior day's excitement. "So, yesterday we got a visit from a couple of guys I saw the same day my Camaro got taken…"

After some embellishment, deflection of blame, and omission of embarrassing details, Bud said, "Well, that's about it. Herb's out getting parts to get the security system going again."

"Wow," said Frank. "Cops and federal agents are watching our cash factory?"

"Those dudes aren't feds," Bud assured him. "Our shit is 100 percent legit, bro."

Frank put a hand on his shoulder. "Yeah, but it will still cost us a boatload to get it straight, if they decide to fuck with us."

"I think the thing we should worry about most – that cop is Lilly's father," Bud said.

"Who's that?" said Frank.

"That's the little chick that keeps coming by here looking for you," Bud said.

Frank paused to mull it over. "I'm still drawing a blank. What she look like?"

"A seventeen-year-old version of her mother," Bud said. "Remember, last month, I kept her busy while you and the mom went to 'the store.'"

"Oh yeah, vaguely." Frank grinned. "But it actually sounds like the lil' babe is into you, not me."

"Have you been talking with Herb?" asked Bud. "Because that's what he said."

"No, but he's right," Frank laughed. "Looks like you're in for an ass whooping for something I did, buddy-boy."

"Again," grumbled Bud.

A few hours later, as Frank and Bud applied the finishing touches of paint, Herb arrived.

Bud greeted him with a smile. "Almost done, bro."

Herb responded by examining the handiwork and took a peek behind the dryer. In an unkind tone, he kindly pointed out, "I don't see a fucking vent hose."

Bud wore a meek, yet friendly smile. "You know, it's kinda funny. I went to the hardware store to get a dryer vent-kit, and got a hundred bucks' worth of shit, but I spaced the dang hose."

Herb's voice rose far past his previous unwarranted level. "I cannot believe what a complete waste-case-shithead you are!"

59

Bud held up a hand. "I'll grab one early tomorrow morning, before I do anything else, promise."

"One more day and that's it," Herb said. "Or your idiot ass can haul that crap to the junkyard."

Like a cornered puppy being harassed by a herd of caffeinated preschoolers, Bud snapped, "Why you always treating me like a bitch?"

"Because you are a bitch," Herb hollered.

"I may be a bitch, but I'm not your bitch," Bud shouted. "So chill, mo-fo!"

The two stood locked in angry stare-down mode for what seemed like an hour, until Frank broke the spell. "Yo, Herb, when do we start work on the Love Bus?"

Herb took a step back and managed a half-smile. "We can start the tear-down first thing tomorrow. We need to lay everything out in the workshop, take measurements, and make a preliminary list before we do anything else."

Bud asked, "How long do you think this build is gonna take?"

"My best estimate for a road-ready prototype is at least a few months," Herb said.

"What the fuck?" Bud threw his arms in the air and stomped his foot. "Then we should wait till I get another car before we go tearing up my Bus. I've got tons of shit to do before you fuck it up."

"I'm not fucking it up," Herb said. "We're improving it."

"I don't care. We're gonna hold off on the demolition till I get me another ride." Bud stomped toward the door. "Well, that's all the bullshit I can deal with today; looks like I'm outta here, dick."

Herb tried the friendly approach. "Hey, wait, dude. Where you going? I bought tons of electronics. C'mon, man. Get over it and stay here to help me fix the system."

Bud didn't look back. Instead, he raised the volume a few notches. "I've been working all fuckin' day, so you're on your own. You got twenty minutes to get anything out of it you need. I'm going to the titty bar. Don't wait up."

Unable to comprehend why five seconds of civility did not soothe his friend, Herb screamed at the closing door, "You better fix that vent hose tomorrow. Or you're history, dude."

# 6

The next day, Bud lay in bed for hours, enjoying a massive thunderstorm rumbling and booming overhead at window-rattling intensity.

He managed to break himself from the trance about half past noon and wandered downstairs to face Herb.

Bud smiled when he opened the door to an empty kickback room.

After his morning ritual, or three, he scrambled up some breakfast to go with his toast.

Around two in the afternoon, he decided it was about time to make up with Herb and set off for the workshop to get it over with. When he opened the garage door, he got an eyeful of VW Bus torn into hundreds of pieces littering the floor along the side wall. He hollered, "FUUUUUCK!!!"

After a frozen period of sullenly staring at the carnage, Bud shook his head and grumble-sighed, "Fuckers. That's the most fucked-up-shit they ever did. I wonder where the hell those asswipes are."

It took him several minutes to gather the will to convince his legs to take him away. As he moved along, Bud kicked an imaginary soccer ball a few times, imagining the ball was Herb's head. He booted the ball over a fence when he discovered the note on a stool next to the drafting table: "FIX THE VENTHOSE MORON!"

Bud screamed to the Heavens, "Fuckin' dickheads, I can't believe this crap! They better put my van back together or I'll make them eat my... Fuck it, no point stressing. Better just get to work on that damn dryer exhaust so I can get the fuck out of this fuckin' place."

Bud took a break to calm and motivate himself and left the room before the smoke cleared. He returned with a basketful of filthy towels and swung it up onto the dryer, lifted the washer's lid, measured in some detergent, began the fill-up cycle, tossed in the towels, and closed the lid to get it started.

After another brief break to replenish THC levels within the fatty acids on top of his brain, he stepped out once again and returned to the couch with clipboard in hand. During his fifteen minutes of scribbling here and there, he ripped three more mighty bowls.

He jumped up and shouted, "Fuckers!" and then stomped over to set the clipboard on the dryer. He grabbed a firm hold of the appliance with both hands and slid it forward while spinning it a quarter turn, exposing its backside.

He traveled back and forth to the workshop several times to grab tools, two spools of electrical wire, a cathode, an anode, different types of hoses – vent, water, gas, conduit – a propane tank, plus a whole slew of other crap.

Fifteen minutes later, the tools and supplies were strewn about near the dryer.

Bud then spent more than an hour head scratching, bong hitting, and, most important of all, rigging all that stuff to the back of the dryer. The finished configuration was a semi-tidy tangle of hoses, wires, splitters, couplings, and tank. After twice giving it the once-over, he declared, "That should be that – two in the tank, one to the grow room. Problem solved, fucker!"

Bud tossed the clean, wet towels into the dryer and set the cycle in motion. After a few minutes of heat build-up, steam began escaping from the hose-couplings, so he yanked the door open.

With palms on cheeks and elbows resting on the dryer, he pored over his notes. Every so often, he flipped back and forth through pages, scribbled a note, then scratched his head with the back of the pen.

Bud stood up straight. "Wait, I got it."

He checked the wiring with an electrical tester, and the needle did not budge. Bud smiled. "Duh, that's why. No power."

He scratched his ass, grabbed his clipboard, and went zombie-like to plop back onto the couch for a few. A mighty smoke cloud remained swirling overhead as he once again sprang to his feet and scurried out to the workshop.

He returned with a small transformer and proceeded to wire it into the dryer's tangled jumble. The instant the transformer's plug slid into the wall outlet, the overhead lights flickered and flashed before the room went dark.

Bud yanked the plug from the wall and screeched, "Damn, what the fuck did I do now?" Those words just past his lips, and engulfed in a sea of pitch black, a massive thunder clap boomed directly overhead. He lurched toward the front door.

Then he laughed. "Fuckin' scared me. Guess it's just a blackout."

After feeling his way to the couch, there was light from his lighter.

The power outage was short lived, but the lights came back on accompanied by a shower of sparks originating from the backside of the dryer. In a flash, those sparks burst into flame. Bud launched from the couch with bong in hand and dumped the old muddy water to kill the flames.

The bong water did the trick, and he got to it so fast that there was no serious damage. But it stunk worse than a skunk with explosive diarrhea.

After a thorough cleaning of the area, the stench of burnt electrical bong water still owned the breathable air. Tired of mouth breathing, Bud began dousing the area with every kind of air freshener he could locate, but it still reeked worse than a homeless junkie whose only sustenance was Night Train and refried beans.

He doused the entire vicinity with baking soda, which caused a chemical reaction with the deodorants' residue and the jumble of hoses and wiring began to foam and smoke. But then it was over. And something beautiful happened – the chemical reaction neutralized the odor.

Bud kept a nose on the situation for a few minutes and then, satisfied that the place no longer smelled like New Jersey, said, "Where was I? Oh yeah, the dryer."

He restarted the cycle. After the dryer heated up, Bud roughly tugged, pushed, pulled, and shook the jumble to make sure that there was no steam where it should not be.

He kept a watchful eye for ten minutes straight, all the while repeating his rough-tug-abuse test several times; still no steam. Bud fist pumped and growled, "Great, I guess my idea works. Fuck you, Herb. As far as you know, I did it your way, bitch!"

To add a fine finish, he encased the hose-wiring tangle with black duct tape then shoved the dryer back into its spot.

He stuck two middle fingers in the air. "Fuck you, fuckers!"

A few hours later, Frank and Herb returned. Bud greeted them with a savage puppy-dog-frown and yipped, "I finished the fuckin' dryer vent, so you fuckers better put my Bus back together."

Herb gave a quick glance toward the dryer. "That wasn't so difficult, now was it?"

"Whatever," said Bud, and then he cranked up the volume several notches. "What about my Bus, fucker?"

"I told you we were going to start the demolition today," Herb said. "You disappeared last night, so we started on the project without you."

Frank grinned. "Yeah, we got started real early, cursing you and tearing up your ride. Actually, I did most of the tearing shit up. He cursed. Then I made him take me to the strip joint for pitchers."

"That is what you get for being irresponsible," said Herb, wearing a crooked smirk.

"Yeah, whatever, dick," Bud said. "What I meant to say was, tomorrow morning you two assholes will help me rebuild it. You'll never know how much I regret suggesting my Bus."

"But you did, and we already started," said Herb.

"Bullshit!" Bud screamed. "This whole alternative-fuel thing is Herb's idea, so get another car."

"I have to admit, I'm totally with Herb on this one," Frank said. "Your V-Dub is perfect. And the most perfect part is it's already in pieces waiting to be reborn and once again save the world." He laughed. "Plus, way easier tearing shit apart than building it up."

"I'm really sorry," Herb said. "It'll be easy to score another canvas, if you really want me to. But your Bus is perfect on so many levels."

Herb's apology, rarer than a semi-honest politician, knocked Bud off his anger and into a void of silent stupor.

Herb seized the opening by patting him on the shoulder while smiling like someone bargaining to be allowed to insert just the tip. "It's your fault, dude. That awesome sketch sealed the deal for me."

Unaware of how to deal with praise, Bud folded quicker than a kite in a hurricane. "Well, I guess," he mumbled, "but what am I going to do for a car?"

"We can find you something to drive until the Bus is running on weed," Herb said. "Then your silly ass can roam about the land showing off my alternative-fuel vehicle."

Bud shrugged. "Yeah, but who knows when that'll be?"

"All I need are a few chassis and wheel-base measurements, and then I can order all the preliminary supplies for you two to get started," Herb said. "While I'm waiting for that stuff, I can run various computations on hemp's chemical properties and get an energy output baseline."

"You don't have to tear it apart for those measurements," Bud said, "and you still didn't say how long it's gonna fuckin' take."

Herb apparently no longer felt like smiling. "It will probably take a few weeks until I have an idea of the best direction to take, and from that point I will have a much more accurate picture of our timetable."

"That's great," Bud said. "Sounds like you won't need me for a while."

The time for diplomacy evaporated into the recent past, so Herb barked, "I need your help, so don't make any plans, asshole."

Bud socked him in the junk. "Well, I'm gonna take off, dick."

# 7

For an entire week, except for an occasional "fucker," "dick," or "asshole" mumbled in passing, Bud and Herb did not have much to say to one another. So Herb toiled away in brainstorm mode out in the workshop, and Bud did his thing wherever Herb was not.

That all changed one afternoon when Herb came up with "a very promising idea," leading to loads of excitement, planning, and considerable begging of Bud to "Get over it, man."

Bud had neglected to mention that he was no longer angry about the "whole bullshit alternative-energy bullshit." In fact, he was raring to get going on the build. The change of attitude arrived at the exact moment he came up with his own creative automotive project for using the leftover Bus parts.

So instead of being bitchy and difficult, Bud awoke early the next day as Herb requested. Ready to set sail, he plopped onto the couch and loaded up the Weeble to begin his daily wobble. One problem: no lighter.

Bud went to the kitchen and rifled through then slammed shut every drawer and cupboard. No lighter or match could be found. After the flurry of exploration, he spun on his heels and spent a few moments with eyes locked onto the stove.

He turned to leave, but halted in his tracks to glance back over his shoulder, and then shrugged. "What the hell. It's worth a try."

Bud brought bong to stove, cranked the knob corresponding to the front left burner, watched, waited, and gazed lovingly at the bong's bowl a few times. Then he began twisting his torso in a way to keep the bowl in ignition position without spilling stinky water. Ever so close, but not quite there, Bud twisted even further to contort like a Russian gymnast auditioning for a gay porno. No dice.

He attempted a few more assorted angles of attack before surrendering with a whimper. "Fuckin' electric stoves are useless! Fuck it, I'll just get some papers and roll a fatty. Now, where the hell are those EZ Triple Widers at?"

Bud searched high and low. But like his fruitless quest for fire, the hunt for rolling papyrus proved just as elusive. He stood staring at the bong, wiped a tear from his eye, and admonished himself. "Think, idiot. If I was rolling papers, where would I be?"

The papers refused to channel themselves through Bud, so he remained locked in a trance until a smile exploded across his face. "That's perfect."

He made a brief trip to the workshop and returned with a handheld propane torch. After opening the valve and clicking the igniter's flint a few times, it did not light.

Bud held the tip near his ear, but nothing was flowing. "Fuuuuuuuuuuuck," he whined.

More than twenty minutes since he woke up, Bud began jonesing even harder. Then in between a blink of a heartbeat –

bam! – his eyes shot open wide as if a bell had rung. He spun a hundred eighty degrees, sprinted toward the dryer, opened the vented doors, and from the bottom shelf retrieved a canister almost identical to his empty propane tank.

He fumbled about, disconnecting the tank, and let the coupling fall from his hand, then launched it back into the cubby with his toe. Bud scurried to the dining table to install the torch tip onto the second tank. When he turned the valve, the sound of hissing gas made him smile. He clicked the igniter and that shit lit.

Bud howled, "Hell yeah! Who's your daddy, beotch?"

After snapping the long-desired bong hit and holding in the smoke long enough for his toe-knuckle hairs to shimmy, once again it was breathing time. Advancing one hit nearer to temporary satisfaction drew a goofy, green-inspired grin.

Bud demolished six more hits in rapid-fire succession, and then disconnected the welding attachment, reinstalled the tank, and returned the propane torch to the workshop.

When he got back, Herb stood with his arms crossed and bitched, "I'm tired of always waiting around for you. Are you ready to get to work on the Love Bus?"

"Right on," Bud smiled. "Let's get at it, bro."

By the time Bud made it out to the workshop, Herb was at his computer and focused on scribbling into a workbook.

Bud looked over his shoulder. "Bro, it's been two weeks, and I still have no idea how you plan to make this shit work."

Herb did not turn around.

"Yo, bro," Bud grumbled. "Give me some answers or I'm out of here!"

Herb continued scribbling, while also pleading, "Dude, don't go. All I need is a minute for the computer to boot up and sign onto the network. Then I'll be happy to explain my new idea and what I need from you."

Bud went to a stool at the far end of the work bench and then watched him work for a few moments. But not that long. "Hey, Herb, if you don't need me, I got shit I wanna do."

Herb ignored him, except for a quick finger flip indicating it would be one minute.

Sixty-eight seconds later, Bud said, "Times up, fucker."

Herb peeled his eyes from the monitor and set down his pen. "Okay, dude, I'm almost positive that I'm onto a way of making that old Bus operate on cannabis power."

"That's great," Bud said with furrowed brow. "But I don't get it. If all we're gonna do is make it run on a different fuel, why did you guys tear my Bus into a gazillion pieces?"

"We didn't really need to," Herb said. "I was just pissed off at you for running off."

The smile fell from Bud's face. He drew a deep breath, readying for rage.

Before Bud could explode, Herb cracked up. "Just kidding, dude. Calm down. We had to."

"I guess," Bud grumbled with a shrug. "But, do you even have any idea how this shit's gonna work?"

Herb gazed off into the vast dream-space of future's promise, which twinkled in his eye as he spoke. "There are so many different ideas twirling and tumbling around in my head, twenty-four hours of every day, it overwhelms. So far, my research points to at least three approaches toward my game-changer, new-paradigm, twenty-first-century fueling breakthrough. All I have to do is settle on one."

"Wuhhhhh?" asked Bud.

Herb rolled his chair out of the way. "Just come over here and check out my designs."

Bud scooted his chair over and took a few notes while digesting the info on the monitor.

Herb gave him almost enough time to soak it all up. "So you see, we'll need to build this from the ground up. I believe the most probable final design will utilize four direct-drive electric motors, with electric steering and brakes. That will eliminate lots of weight."

Bud worked the mouse to zoom in on the CAD image, and then motioned toward the pointer on the screen. "What's this cylinder you've got in the middle of the frame rails?"

"That might be the fuel tank, or even a cooling tank, depending on my final energy conversion method," Herb said. "I haven't completely ruled out a method that burns material for energy. But it must be ultra-efficient, on a magnitude of scale well beyond current technology. Otherwise, what's the point?"

"The V-Dub's frame design is perfect for independent all-wheel drive." Bud moved the cursor in a circle around a section of the schematic. "You got the side rails right, but you left out the five cross members. So your tank would have to sit on top of them."

"We'll just relocate it to the engine compartment," Herb said.

"Too small, bad weight distribution, and way too much work to end up with a half-ass fix," Bud chuckled. "Hey, is there gonna be three octane grades of fuel – dirt, stress, and chronic?"

Herb shook his head. "Probably not..." He stopped to eyeball Bud for a moment before scribbling a note. "Actually, that is a great question, man. I'll run a model to assess any fluctuations of marijuana's plant protein energy output levels in different strains. If there's a difference, I will program some preset parameters into the vehicle's control module."

Bud tilted back in his chair and smiled. "That's awesome, bro, but what do you need for me to do – right here and right now – that I had to wake up for two hours ago? I need to get done in here and take care of the lack of fire-creating devices in the crib."

"For starters, while I am running the numbers and researching the chemistry," Herb said, "I need you to assess every possible way to reduce gross weight of the finished vehicle. Then give me a written report of your findings and suggestions."

"I'll just take a few notes and tell you what I've got," Bud said. "Then if you want a written report, you can write that shit down as I dictate."

Herb shrugged. "I guess that will be fine, but let's get to it."

Bud waved an arm toward the CAD image. "I can tell you right now, if we're gonna build it all-wheel drive, with independent suspension, add that huge tank thingy, and wind up lighter than OEM, we'll need to fabricate a titanium frame. Plus, that way I get to use my new TIG welder, which totally kicks ass!"

The instant he heard "titanium," Herb got busy searching a technical database. After a few moments of darting eyeballs and digesting information, he said, "Wow, titanium has a two-to-one strength-to-weight ratio compared to steel, with an unbelievable tensile strength. We can build a far superior frame, stronger than the original, and it would only weigh half as much. For sure, let's build another frame."

Bud shook his head, smiled, patted Herb on the shoulder, and asked, "Do we need the old drivetrain for anything?"

"I don't think so, why?" asked Herb.

Bud erupted into full-on arm-flailing mode, words exiting his brain so fast they tripped over one another. "Well, if I took the old 1700 motor, slapped on a set of dual Webbers and some headers, it would make a sweet motor. Maybe get a hundred thirty or more horses. I can change the gearing in the stock tranny for nothing, and use the steering and brake stuff, too. Then all I'll need is some fat tires, a kick-ass-suspension, and I'm set."

"Slow down," Herb said. "Set for what?"

"I figure if I'm gonna build a frame for your project vehicle, I might as well build a dune buggy frame, too. That way I can put the old drivetrain stuff to work. Buy a kick-ass fiberglass tub..."

Herb cut him off. "You know, I bet this world is a far safer place without your ever-stoned ass operating a motor vehicle along our nation's highways and byways."

"You're wrong, man," Bud scoffed. "I'm a super-safe driver, because pot makes me drive real slow-like. Plus, I know that the left lane is for passing, so I stay in the right lane and out of people's way, minding my own business. But the most important reason of all – marijuana cures road rage, bro."

Herb rolled his eyes. "Sure it does, dude."

"Seriously, bro." Bud placed his hands on an invisible steering wheel and looked straight ahead. "Say I'm driving around and haven't smoked any weed all fuckin' day long. When some asshole cuts me off nasty – or any of a zillion other dumbass things drivers do – I'd want to run him off the road into a parked car or some other wicked-cool-wrong shit like that. But when I'm buzzed, I just tool along, 'do-do-do-do-do.' Then, when that inevitable idiot comes ass-holing along, I smile and pretend like I didn't even notice the dis. I must have saved hundreds of lives and thousands in legal fees. And so far, fucker, I haven't killed you. That's proof it works."

Herb remained expressionless. "Very funny, but what about all the stupid mistakes stoned drivers make?"

"Rookies, man," said Bud with a cocky grin. "Hey, enough of that shit. What do you need me to do right now?"

"I made a checklist." Herb flipped back and forth through his notebook. "Yeah, here it is. Tidy up the work area and throw out all the junk we have no use for. When you're done with that, make me a list of needed supplies so I can put in the purchase orders."

Bud turned and waved an arm toward the other side of the shop. "Have you taken a look behind you lately?"

Herb swiveled his chair and discovered a very tidy scene less than thirty feet away. "Wait, when did you do all that?"

Bud chuckled a bit then laid out the layout. "Frank and me been moving that shit around for days. The frame and body are outside covered with tarps. The drivetrain is up on blocks over there." He pointed to the doors lining the far wall. "Those will be out of the way there. That pile by the rollup is most likely trash. Dumpster's full."

Herb shook his head and shrugged. "Well that's all fine and dandy, but you still need to drain the oil from the engine and transmission so they won't leak on my floor. Then take the fluids for recycling."

"Already done, bro." Bud smiled. "I also got rid of the gas from the tank, bitch. According to what you said earlier, all that's left for me today is making a supplies list. Oh yeah, you need to print out those plans for me, too."

Herb once again surveyed the work area, and then scratched his head. "Alright, I guess. But be ready to work first thing Monday morning."

Bud jotted notes double-time onto a legal pad, and less than three minutes later ripped the sheet from the pad. "Here's your list, dickhead. I could've slept in and wrote this shit from the couch. Oh yeah, I bet titanium will be harsh on my tools, so triple up on the drill bits, grinders, blades and abrasive paper."

Herb made a note, then gave the list the once over. "You haven't written down any design ideas."

"I told ya. That's on you." Bud tossed the pen onto the table. "Start writing quick, mofo. Once I build the new frame, I'm gonna fabricate carbon fiber doors. But I'll make the front door openings bigger, and they'll open gull-wing style. We'll get rid of the side sliding door and make the back door roll up into the roof."

"That sounds like a whole lot of extra work," Herb said.

Bud shrugged. "Maybe, but you're paying. Plus it'll give me something fun to do instead of sitting around here work-waiting for you to figure out your next move, Tesla."

"Very funny," Herb scoffed. "I've only brainstormed for two weeks, and I am quite confident that my progress will exceed your ability to keep up."

"Sure you are, bro," said Bud. "I'm going to build me a dune buggy, too. I put the stock for it on the list."

"Sure you are, dude," Herb parroted. "So how long do you think it would take to build the frame, attach the body, and do that door fabrication?"

"I think once we get the supplies, Frank and me can build both frames, plus reconfigure the unibody ready for the doors, in about two weeks; maybe three because of quagmires. And after that, while you're waiting and figuring out all your slow shit, I can do all my tricked-out stuff building a better buggy."

"How long do you think it would take – you know – if you concentrate on the task at hand and build only one frame?" Herb sniveled.

Bud counted on fingers, stopped to jot a note, then resumed counting while mumbling to himself, "Two, carry the five and... yeah, that's about – well maybe if I... no. Yeah, that should work." He stopped his mental math and grinned. "We could get that shit done in ten, maybe twelve weeks."

"Touché," said Herb. "I think two or three weeks sounds better. So, I guess that's it."

"Right on, bro," Bud patted him on the back. "Don't stress out so much, we'll get this shit rockin' in no time!"

"We shall see," Herb grumbled. "Do me a favor. Try not to plan any other sidetrack projects."

"Well, seems like I'm done for today," Bud said with a smile. "I got a sidetrack already planned for inside. C-ya!"

"Okay, dude," Herb said. "But make sure that's the last one."

Before he left, Bud went shopping in the supply room. He threw a T-valve, the propane torch tip, various hand tools, fasteners, and doodads into a tool bag, and then grabbed a roll of quarter-inch gas hose and set off for the kick-back area.

Once inside, Bud let the tool bag drop to his side, tossed the hose onto the dryer, and then turned facing the Weeble-Bong to proclaim, "Now the lovingly pungent bongload shall always have the flame of life to set it ablaze. I will be the master of the stoner universe."

He smiled like one having their balls tickled by a feather-wielding super model. "I have onc-upped you, Weeble Bong."

With a glide in his stride and some chips in his dip, Bud got busy on his side-trip. He slid the couches and tables away and cleared a path to the laundry area. Then he removed the baseboard trim all the way to where the corner table had resided. Next, he retrieved the gas hose and flung it out toward the dryer and then wedged the hose into the vacant space between the bottom of the drywall and the foundation until he arrived back in the laundry area.

After knocking the trim back into place, Bud retrieved the gas canister from the lower shelf beside the dryer, disconnected the gas supply, and connected the T-valve. One of the valve's outputs was for the hose he just ran along the wall, and the second sent gas to its original destination.

Once all the furniture arrived back home, Bud bounced onto the couch and attached a welding tip to the hose. All set and ready to rip, he loaded an extra-large bowl of sticky-green salvation and turned the valve while activating the igniter. Presto change-o, flame appeared.

Bud hollered, "I'm king of the world!"

His high-ness proceeded to take seven bong rips in under ten minutes.

After a relaxing vegetative-meditation, he peeled his ass from the couch to gather up all the tools and leftover supplies. When he was halfway to the workshop, the door buzzer sounded. On the monitor, Frank stood at the front door.

Bud elbowed the speakerphone mounted on the hallway wall. "Come on in, bro, I'll be back up front in a second." He buzzed the door lock and then continued on down the hall.

Bud hurried back to share a boisterous boast. "Dude, I just took five rips in less than five minutes."

"That's great," Frank said, backside to couch with loaded bong in hand. "I would love to join you on your journey, but I can't seem to find a lighter."

"Funny you should ask, for I have solved the fire problem forever." Bud grinned then demonstrated the proper operation of his brand-spanking-new bong lighter, in conjunction with a virtually spill-proof water-pipe, by taking Frank's hit and blowing a thick plume of sweet nostril-teasing smoke into his face.

"Good for you, fucker." Frank laughed then killed a bong hit, then another, and then one more before giving up. "Dude, I'm already fucked up. There's no way you took five hits of this shit in five minutes."

Bud nodded. "Yup."

Frank held up the torch tip. "Hey, where's the other end of the hose connected?"

Bud pointed to the dryer. "Over there, bro."

"You're running this contraption with natural gas?" Frank asked.

"Not exactly; that's an electric dryer. But there's a gas source over there." Bud looked down the hall to the front door, and then made a quick check of the video monitors before continuing in a hushed tone, "Herb didn't want me to do it. But I've been welding since I was ten, and I know how to connect gas hoses. So it's safe. But just in case, don't mention it to him. I'll deal with him if he asks."

"Where is Herb?" asked Frank.

"He's in the workshop, thinking his brains out while we're smoking our brains out," Bud said. "Been there all day figuring out how to make my Bus run on weed. I wish he'd have figured that shit out before you two tore my baby apart."

Frank sat up straight, smiled, and tossed Bud a video-game controller. "I believe the time has come for an all-out Madden battle royale."

"Right on, bro," Bud said. "But promise me one thing. Don't cry out loud when I humiliate your ass."

"Did you stock up on Gerber's?" Frank chuckled. "Because you're gonna win the big-baby prize tonight, dude."

Frank and Bud set to gaming in earnest, grouching, yelling, and talking endless shit. Turns out, Bud was so low that he had to "look up to see down." And, apparently, Frank's momma had "more clap than an auditorium."

Three hours later, Herb wandered in from his shop with red, knuckle-imprinted cheeks and his hair more tangled than a box full of extension cords.

"Hey, bro," Bud said. "It's about time. You make your breakthrough?"

Herb dropped onto the couch. "Almost, but I just cannot figure out the last, tiny, critical step. Every time I think I'm there, the numbers just don't stand up under scrutiny." He glanced to the clock. "Wow, 11:15. I haven't smoked all day."

"Allow me." Frank passed the loaded bong, smiled, and lit that shit for him.

Happiness is a warm bong, so Herb exhaled and smiled.

Bud reloaded the Weeble and handed it back. "Here, take another rip, bro."

After receiving the newly installed flammable appliance, Herb tugged on the hose. "Where does this come from?"

"A little something Bud came up with," said Frank.

The blood drained from Herb's face. "Oh no!" He bolted straight up in his seat, shut the valve, and began a higher level of scrutiny, trying to determine the hose's source beyond the corner table.

Frank gave Bud a quick wink. "It's alright. I helped him do it."

Bud smiled. "Yeah, he helped alright."

Herb spent a few seconds pondering, then gave in and set the appliance down. It did not take long for him to settle back deep into the couch, and, while battling to keep eyelids from shutting completely, he mumbled, "I guess it's probably safe, then."

"Hey, I got some good news." Bud grinned like a dog eating peanut butter. "I dominated Frank, eight Madden tournaments in a row, so I own his two-left-thumbed ass for at least as long as it takes to build our frames. We will start as soon as you get the goods. It's all on you now, bro."

"Sounds good." Herb smiled. "I'm pretty sure I will have settled on an acceptable conversion technology by then. We shall see if between your sidetracks and vidiot-tournaments, you two buffoons can keep pace with me."

"I know what you need to get your creative juices flowing," Bud said. "You need to smoke some pot while you work. Talk about converting weed into useful energy."

"I am far too responsible to waste my time like that," Herb grumbled. "I would never get a thing done. Besides, people who wake and bake – and bake – and bake spend all their free time figuring out how to keep a bong lit."

"Dude, I helped you all I could today." Bud held up the bong lighter. "Then I spent the rest of the day on my creative project, which I might add was an utter success." He laughed. "Plus, I maintained an incredibly pleasing level of being fuuucked up all day, beotch."

Herb shook his head slowly. "Trust me. You two will never realize your true potential while being slaves to weed."

"I disagree," Frank said. "When it comes to trust, I believe what a Buddhist friend once told me: 'Trust no one. Educate yourself. Read everything. Listen to the masters. But when you're through searching, ignore everything you read and all the advice of the gurus unless it makes sense for you. Even if you must stand alone against the crowd, trust only yourself.'"

# 8

While Herb slaved away at his computer for an entire two months, he grew ever more frustrated at his inability to achieve even the slightest success toward his goal.

But while Herb was coming up blank, Frank and Bud had managed to complete a tremendous amount of work on the Love Bus. During that time, they fabricated a feather-light, ultra-strong titanium frame for the Love Bus and also built a dune buggy frame. Then they got busy modifying the Bus' unibody by chopping the top and widening the front door openings by fourteen inches. After attaching it to the new frame, they went to work inside to construct a titanium skeleton for mounting the gull-wing doors. As soon as the motors and wiring supplies arrived, the new doors that were already built could be installed in about a day.

They also sanded the entire body smoother than a baby's butt and then covered it with carbon fiber. After the carbon fiber cured completely, they moved back inside and reduced even more weight by jettisoning all non-essential interior body parts, leaving only a third of the Bus' original metal skin remaining underneath the new shell. With nothing left to do, the doorless, wheel-less Bus shell remained resting atop five railroad ties, allowing the guys to set off in earnest on Bud's dune buggy build.

After another long day of scouring the city for "the coolest fiberglass buggy tub ever," Frank and Bud returned home to the kickback area for cerebral nourishment.

Herb came in from the shop and shook his head while staring disapprovingly, just as Bud licked the paper's gummed edge and then slid a finger along the doobie's seam.

Satisfied that his newest creation was ready for trial by fire, Bud presented the perfectly rolled object of the crowd's hopes and desires and smiled. "All done."

In preparation for some vigorous pot smoking, Frank sat up straight and then gave a light golf clap. "Light it up, buddy."

Bud placed joint to lips, and, with the simple push of a button, activated the recently installed BongRiteEternalFlame – the torch-tip lighter thingy, renamed and vastly improved to address numerous safety and ease-of-use concerns – and the doobie roared to life in a blaze of glory.

Frank shook his head and smiled wide while heaping on another helping of unrelenting praise. "Dude, your EternalFlame has got to be the greatest invention ever. You have foiled lighter thieves once and for all."

With a slight puff out of his chest, Bud smiled. "That was the plan."

"Just wait until I get the Love Bus completed," Herb sneered. "Then you will see useful. Change-the-world useful, I might add."

"Yeah, about that," Frank said. "Make any breakthroughs since this morning?"

Herb straightened up out of his slouch and un-frowned. "Actually, yes. I had a very promising idea right after you knuckleheads split, when I suddenly realized that I need to tackle this question from a whole new angle – think outside the box."

Frank grinned. "You're going to run the Love Bus on clichés?"

Bud said, "Bro, Jack in the Box sounds good right now."

"Thinking inside the box for dinner, huh?" said Frank.

Herb scowled and grumbled, "Are you two blockheads done? I'm trying to explain about how, after crunching numbers and computer modeling for most of today, I'm positive that I am onto something big."

Frank got a huge smile and offered the joint. "That's awesome."

Herb left him hanging. "None for me. I've decided to keep my mind clear until I get through this project."

Frank and Bud broke up in stitches.

"You two should try it," Herb screeched. "Maybe then you guys will help me out in the shop more, instead of staying constantly baked."

"Don't be such a ball-buster." Frank waved an arm in the direction of the workshop. "We've been kicking major ass for months, plus we've done all we can do until that drivetrain shit gets here."

"Fair enough," Herb said, while making an awful attempt at a smile. "I have good news on that front, too. I spoke with Twenty-Four-Seven Wholesale Electronics, and they assured me that my parts will be here this week."

"I'll believe it when I see it," said Bud.

Frank bolted to his feet. "All that shit's lovely, but I think at this very minute the most pressing matter is that me and Bud go get sixteen tacos."

"Grab me a Jumbo Jack and a chocolate shake," Herb said. "I have to get back to the workshop. I just came in here to tell you chucklehead-wasteoids that I've got something big brewing, and will need your undivided attention for the next few weeks."

# 9

Five days later, Frank and Bud had only managed a half day's worth of Love Bus wrenching. Not for lack of want, but because most of the necessary parts were yet to arrive.

Despite that, Herb still bitched and moaned and demanded they stick close by, because "any minute now," the long-anticipated delivery would happen. And he was "right on the verge of something big."

Because they were having tons of fun tinkering on the dune buggy, Frank and Bud offered only token resistance. That particular day, they were kicking back in the buggy's bucket seats resting upon the floor amongst scattered auto parts, killing time and brain cells with their favorite mental medicinal.

As usual, Herb sat across the shop, glued to his computer, slaving away with calculations, building conceptual models and scribbling notes; fail, rinse, repeat.

Bud yelled across the workshop, "Figure out anything yet, Newton?"

Herb did not reply.

Bud shouted a little louder, "Dude, it's like I been tellin' ya, come over here and smoke some pot so you can think more clearly. It'll help you focus and ignore distractions."

Herb turned halfway around to screech, "You're my fucking distraction, and I've been trying to ignore you since high school! Thus far, no amount of weed has helped."

Bud flipped him off and mumbled, "You're wrong, dude."

The sign language drew Herb to turn and face them for a full-throated response. "I'm trying to make a positive difference for the planet, while you waste all your time building bong lighters."

Frank corrected, "Actually, dune buggies and bong lighters, bro."

In the blink of an eye, Herb's backside was all that they saw.

"That'd be a great name for a band." Bud did a head-banging mime and waved the lit EternalFlame high above his head while growling, "'Dune Buggies and Bong Lighters,' waaaaaaah!"

"You should give me one of those," Frank said. "You got them all over this place. Just bring one to my pad."

"Okay, bro, but it's not that simple," Bud said. "But I'll come up with something for ya."

A few minutes later, Bud stood, grinned, motioned for Frank to follow, and whispered, "'Be vewy, vewy quiet. I'm hunting wabbits.'"

They crept toward Herb like big cats stalking small prey. Upon arrival, instead of pouncing, Bud leaned in and blew a massive hit into Herb's face.

At that exact moment, Frank yelled, "BOO, MOTHERFUCKER!"

Herb launched to his feet like a rocket to ruin, stumbled, and gasped in the midst of the wavering cloud. He grabbed onto the desk and steadied himself before bellowing, "Fuck you, Frank – Fuck you, Bud!"

"Sorry, bro, it was an accident." Bud sounded quite sincere. "I tripped and stubbed my toe."

A slight grin suppressed Frank's giggle. "Sorry, man. We didn't plan that shit."

"Please, just leave me the fuck alone," Herb begged.

"I have a great idea," Frank said. "Why don't we all smoke some dope while you update us on everything? Maybe talking about it will reveal a new angle."

"Or a fresh insight," added Bud.

"I just wish you two would quit bugging me every two minutes," Herb whined. "You guys with your fucking bong lighters and dune buggy bullshit. It's a total waste of my time."

"Don't get mad at my success," Bud said. "It's not my fault you decided to make a car that runs on weed, but won't even smoke out while you're trying to solve that problem. I'm sorry, but that shit sounds totally idiotic to me."

Herb waved off the joint. "There is absolutely no correlation between me clogging my brain with cannabis and unleashing potential energy stored within marijuana's molecular structure."

"That's not what I meant," Bud said. "Just sayin', lack of weed makes you more of an ass than usual."

Herb hollered, "I can assure you I wouldn't get a damn thing done if I smoked pot all day. You're so high all the time, you don't even realize how unimportant the things you do are."

"Harsh," said Frank.

Bud took a massive hit, and then with brilliant timing exhaled straight into Herb's face as he inhaled.

Frank and Bud stood and watched while the smoke dissipated. No rant or nothing from Herb; just a sigh and then a much softer tone. "You're right, Frank. That was harsh. I'm sorry, Bud. Some of the stuff you do is useful. The misery caused by events far beyond my control and lack of progress on my project is ultra-frustrating."

Herb locked focus onto the burning joint. "Right on, give me a hit."

Bud smiled and passed the doobie, then danced in circles with arms high in the air like Rocky Balboa.

Before Herb could hit it, the joint went out. Not a problem; Bud activated a nearby EternalFlame to re-ignite the good times. Like an old pro remounting a bicycle that he had fallen off of mere seconds earlier, Herb took a ginormous toke. After holding in the output from one fine sativa for about a minute, he took his sweet time exhaling.

Herb replicated his experimentation. Once again, it delivered the same cloudy results. He rolled the EternalFlame over and back in his hand, clicked the trigger, and appeared hypnotized watching the flame. "This bong lighter device is actually pretty cool, dude."

Bud smiled. "Thanks, man."

Most of the tension having evaporated, Herb turned into their long-lost chum. "Hey, Frank. I appreciate your help, too. I hope you realize that."

Frank nodded. "For sure, buddy."

"I hate to admit it, but you guys were right," Herb said. "I feel 100 percent better." Then with a crooked smile, he tried improving on 100 percent by sucking in another hearty hit.

Bud gave him a soft pat on the back – not in a gay way, but close – and let his hand rest there. "I'm sorry, too, bro. I didn't mean all that stuff I said about idiotic either; just most of it." He chuckled. "But why don't you like my dune buggy plan?"

"Well, to be honest," Herb said, "I haven't been paying attention to your 'dune buggy plan.' What exactly is it, dude?"

Bud turned to face the other side of the workshop and waved an arm toward the far wall. "You're telling me that you haven't noticed my halfway-finished dune buggy?"

Herb scratched his head, rubbed his eyes, and began shuffling his feet toward the Love Bus. To its right, resting atop railroad ties, sat the titanium chassis of an emerging dune buggy. Next to it, the motor and transmission hung from a cherry-picker. Most of the other parts needed to complete the buggy were stacked in boxes or leaning against the wall next to a sparkly-purple fiberglass buggy tub.

A dumfounded Herb stood staring at buggy stuff. "Have you been working on that while I was out?"

Bud shook his head and laughed like a giddy four-year-old being tickled by grandpa. "And I'm the space-brain, huh, fucker? You've been here most of the time we built that buggy, and there's no way we could've knocked out that much shit during the six hours a day you're not in here."

"I must have thought you guys were working on the Love Bus," Herb said. "It obstructs my view."

"Bro, you know we ran out of work on the Love Bus days ago," Bud said. "Plus, I've been telling your supposedly genius ass for months about the kickass buggy I'm building." Bud raised his voice and pointed. "RIGHT fuckin' THERE!"

Herb mumbled, "Maybe I have been working too much." He walked to the beer keg sitting between two bucket seats, masquerading as a table, and kicked it. "Where did this come from? Did you two throw a kegger while I was out?"

Frank laughed. "There's no way that could ever happen. You never leave here long enough for us to have any real fun. Otherwise this place would be a skate park."

"I'm gonna use it as the gas tank for my buggy," Bud said.

Herb's smile faded quicker than blue jeans in a bucket of bleach. He grabbed ahold of the keg and gave it a couple good shakes. "Making a gasoline tank out of an empty beer keg sounds risky."

"Lots of dune buggies have kegs as gas tanks!" Bud said. "I'm just gonna cut it open, put a NASCAR-approved fuel cell in it, then weld that puppy back together. I like the look; it says 'PAR-TEE' in every language."

"Maybe that's true, but what about this contraption of yours?" Herb went to the nearest EternalFlame. "I admit it's very useful, but I worry about you and gas connections."

"C'mon, dude, that was a one-time thing." Bud scrunched down a bit, looked to the floor, and mumbled, "I learned my lesson about gas safety after your uncle's house got blown to shit. Plus, he's not mad at me anymore, now that the skin grafts are done." He locked eye to eye with Herb. "I didn't use any duct tape at all this time, promise."

Herb clicked the trigger to reignite the doobie. "Either way, I am still quite skeptical about this beer keg as a gas tank, doubly so when it's your idea. I'll research it. First things first, I need to take a look at how you have your little bong lighter contraption rigged up; better safe than sorry."

Herb began reeling gas hose hand over hand to pull himself toward the EternalFlame's ultimate source.

Bud frowned, started to say something, thought better of it, and settled on shadowing Herb's journey of discovery.

Twelve steps into his investigation, an instant message alert from Herb's computer froze him in his tracks. He turned around and obediently went to check it while puffing the doobie like a choo-choo train all the way back to his seat.

Bud let out a big sigh of relief, grinned, and turned to Frank and mouthed, "Saved by the bell."

Frank nodded. "I wonder who that is. It must be pretty important."

Bud shrugged, plopped down into a bucket seat and began preparation of another fat joint. Those two watched Herb toke away, fingers dancing upon the keyboard in double-time, chatting.

"I just thought of something," said Frank.

"What's that?" Bud asked.

Frank pointed. "If we can see Herb from here, then obviously he can see us from his computer. All he would have to do is turn around and he would see your buggy."

"It's pretty pathetic, huh?" Bud laughed. "Building this shit ain't very quiet, either."

"No," Frank said. "Actually I think it's great that he set a goal and gives it his full attention. That kind of determination and concentration is rare."

"I guess." Bud shrugged. "But I think he needs to relax a bit. He's stressing out so much he's probably missing obvious things. Less is more!"

"I agree 100 percent," Frank said. "He needs to take a break – get a hooker or something."

Bud finished the rolling ritual by sliding tongue tip along gummed edge before dragging a fingertip along the seal to make sure it stayed rolled tight. After a brief drying period, he activated the EternalFlame to introduce flame to weed, thus igniting the first joint of the rest of his life.

After they finished the doobie, Frank said, "Let's hit the titty bar."

"Great idea," Bud said. "We'll make Herb come with us."

They both hopped up to head across the workshop and peered over Herb's shoulder as he pounded away on his keyboard like a concert pianist playing Slayer.

"Hey, bro. Me and Frank are going to a go-go – so go-go with us." Bud giggled like a thirty-six-year-old school girl who had been paid extra.

Herb peeled an eye from the screen and smiled. "I have great news…"

Frank cut him off. "You're going to the titty bar with us?"

Herb was nearly breathless. "Can't leave now. I had a brilliant idea earlier and just received confirmation of its viability from my old professor at Tech. He is super excited about my idea. Says it's 'quite promising.' And he wants me to do more research on…"

Frank interrupted him again. "Good idea, let's research how many lap dances it'll take you to find the gorilla of your dreams."

"We're gonna help you find the square of sixty-nine!" Bud chuckled.

Frank grinned. "It's ate-something."

They both cracked up while shoving and slapping Herb on the back.

Herb's tone switched from happy excitement to an annoyed grumble. "One day you two will realize that life is serious, not just some big fucking joke. There is far more to life than getting laid and stumbling around stoned."

"I hope not!" Bud cried out.

Frank offered a careless shrug. "My philosophy of life can be summed up by the words of that Rolling Stones' song."

Herb asked, "Which Stones' song?"

Frank sang, in an almost pleasant tone, like a dinosaur with its throat numbed from a cocaine drip, "'I know, it's all a fuckin' joke. But I like it – like it. Yes I do!'"

Bud corrected him, "Bro, that song is, 'It's Only Rock 'n' Roll.'"

"Wow, seriously?" Frank grinned. "I actually like that better; life is rock 'n' roll!"

"You guys make all the jokes you want," Herb said. "There's more to life than just getting laid by some stripper. I want to find a woman that I can relate to; an intelligent lady who is funny, hard-working, sexy, and sweet."

Herb frowned at how hard the guys laughed.

"You watch too much TV," Frank said. "Does she cook and clean, too?"

"What are you talking about?" Herb asked. "I never watch television."

"More importantly," Bud said, "how does titties and beer sound?"

Herb got his happy smile back. "I think a titty bar is a great idea. Maybe without you guys distracting me, I can further expand my breakthrough."

"Dude, me and Bud had two small fires and built a dune buggy in here," Frank said. "You didn't even get distracted by that shit."

Bud started for the door. "You know where to find us."

Frank was right on his heels.

Herb smiled and yelled at their backsides, "Once I confirm my latest ideas, the project will be back in full gear. There's a 99.9 percent certainty that I will need both of you tomorrow, and until the Love Bus is fully operational."

# 10

As a month trickled past, Herb's promising idea led to several groundbreaking theoretical insights. But to his chagrin, he had yet to discover a viable process for powering the Love Bus on marijuana juice. His 99.9 percent certainty was not as sure a thing as it sounded at the time. Point-one-percent can sure fuck with a scientist, as it did with him and thousands before his time.

In another, lesser quagmire, the drive wheels and electrical components were still not in hand. Even though the Love Bus project remained at a complete standstill, it was not all awful news. Herb achieved some minor success building upon his original energy conversion concept and reportedly had several "stepping stones lined up."

Frank and Bud remained on call at the workshop, ready at a moment's notice to stop buggy building and hop right back into the Love Bus project. Herb would get excited just about every day and shout across the workshop, summoning the guys to tell of an all-important elusive link he just discovered. He'd then say, "It's time to run some real-world experiments."

Whenever Herb explained the details, they did not hold up under the questioning and joke-scrutiny from the stoners who wandered from the far side of his workshop. In most cases, their free humorous evaluations caused Herb to get his pout on while the guys cackled away to leave him to his thinking man's work.

Because it got wicked-cold and damp out in the workshop, Bud also undertook the installation of a pellet-feeder hearth-stove. Herb stayed on his case during the entire project, peering over his shoulder while nonstop moaning about "sidetrack" this and "waste of time" that, all the while insisting they only needed to "wear heavier jackets."

A funny thing occurred once the hearth was up and running – Herb loved it. Winter warmth and nutritious comfort-food – always just a loving ladle away – meant that Herb no longer needed to break away from brainstorming to go inside for nourishment. A kettle of hot and yummy homemade soup simmered on the hearth at all times.

One morning, about half past nine, a sweaty, red-faced Herb bellowed into the phone, "Look, idiot, I told you already: I don't want to be transferred. Last month, you guys fucking promised that I'd have my order within a week. But I've gotten nothing but the runaround since then. And just yesterday, I was assured that I would receive my fucking parts by lunchtime today."

Herb listened as his face twisted into an expression of annoyance verging on vandalistic anger. His voice became loud enough to be heard over a jet taking off. "Are you sure? Well, I'll believe it when I see it, jackass. I'm telling you that stuff better get here today, or you can keep it and cram it up your incompetent shithole." He slammed the receiver down into the cradle so hard it landed on his foot.

Across the way, Frank and Bud were applying some finishing touches on the dune buggy, by sitting in the front seats smoking a fatty. Bud's sparkling purple dune buggy sat parked right next to the Love Bus, which still rested in the same spot it had occupied since the frame and bodywork's completion months before, up on blocks waiting for lots of parts to be semi-complete.

During all their "standby" time, Bud rebuilt the old Bus motor, souped it up with dual carburetors, exhausts, and an upgraded transmission, and then bolted it into his bitchin' buggy. With the finish line in sight, it only took four days to bolt on the tub, bumpers, roll bar, engine cage, beer-keg gas tank, banana buckets, and back seat. The previous night, all the lights, gauges, and wiring got completed. She was ready to roll.

Herb went over to the buggy to report, "The guy said that my parts are on a truck on the way here as we speak."

Bud smiled and gave double thumbs-up. "That's awesome, bro. Now that I'm done with my new ride, it'd be cool to get those parts so we can knock this Love Bus shit out before weed gets legalized."

"Very funny, dude," said an expressionless Herb. "It's not my fault that the parts guys have been jerking my chain."

"It don't matter anyway," Bud said. "Even if we would've had all that crap a month ago, we would've been done in days. The Love Bus would be sitting here on wheels, instead of blocks, while your giant brain figured out something useful to make her go."

Bud hit the doobie and then let the smoke drift lazily from his mouth while offering Herb the joint, which he declined.

"I'm very close," Herb said. "It will happen any day now."

"I'm just busting your chops," Bud said. "I believe in you, man."

Herb managed a slight smile. "Thanks, dude, I appreciate that."

"Right on," Bud said. "Well if the parts are really gonna be here soon, Frank and me are gonna take my buggy out for a shakedown run."

Herb once again declined the offered doobie.

"Dude, I can't believe you're still not partying," Frank said. "Never thought you'd make it a full day, let alone a month, with smokestack Bud belching out never-ending influential clouds of joy."

Bud exhaled one of those happiness clouds toward Herb, timed to hit him straight in his face as he inhaled.

"I plan on staying on the wagon until I complete all experimentation requiring my full critical-reasoning, analysis, and mathematical skills," Herb said. "I must remain sharp and focused."

"They should put seatbelts on wagons," Frank said. "Too many people fall off the wagon. Seatbelts might prevent that."

"Feed your head," Bud chuckled before blowing an even bigger hit into Herb's face.

"I need you guys to be serious for a minute." Herb waved a hole in the smoke cloud hovering around his head. "I want to tell you about a great idea I just had. It's a whole new angle."

Frank grinned like a hyena on hallucinogens. "Can you see the fudge at the end of the tunnel?"

Bud held up a hand to shush him. "Go ahead, bro."

"Well, seeing as the government's giving out huge subsidies to encourage the manufacture of ethanol from corn," Herb said, "maybe I can get in on some of that money. I was thinking of maybe using the sugars from marijuana to produce an ethanol that would cleanly and efficiently power on-demand generators to drive the electric motors. I might run some experiments to see what kind of yield I can get from marijuana-based ethanol."

"That's the stupidest thing I've ever heard, making fuel out of food," Bud said. "I mean, it's cool to drive around. But everyone's got to grub."

Frank frowned. "By that reasoning, making a car to run on weed will burn up a lot more pot, raising prices for the average stoner." In a split second, his frown turned into a grin. "I just realized something. Higher weed prices means 'mo money, mo money, mo money' for us!"

"Sorry to disappoint you," Herb said. "But higher demand would lead to a massive increase in marijuana production, and most likely have a price-lowering effect. Plus, a change in legal status will certainly drive prices even lower."

"Then we should forget about making it run on weed," Frank said. "We should make the Love Bus run on trees, to clear cut as much of that shit as possible. If you design a vehicle that ran on trees, fuckers would be cutting them down just so they could drive to work."

"Quit the bullshit," Herb snarled. "I'm trying to be serious!"

"I'm not kidding," Frank said. "There's a strong case to be made against trees. Without a doubt they're destroying the planet. Think about how many people get killed by trees each year."

Herb groaned, "What the fuck are you talking about, idiot?"

Frank rolled hand over palm up to gesture toward the stand of pines through an imaginary window. "Well, there're all those innocent cars travelling at high speed whose paths get blocked by asshole trees, terrible trees falling on houses and bitch-ass branches dropping on people. That's just the tip of the iceberg. We should focus our efforts on stopping those lumber industry murderers who insist on replanting a tree after each one they have wisely and compassionately chopped down. There is no logical reason to save a tree. We should all consume more timber, paper, and other woodland products to halt this tree scourge once and for all."

"Okay, Rush Limbaugh, you made your funny," Herb said.

"I just realized something; trees grow on trees." Bud chuckled and passed the joint to Herb.

Annoyance and conditioned response demanded that Herb take a puff of pot.

As Herb sucked away like a gay porn star in a dick factory, Bud cheered, "Ah ha – BUSTED!"

After a long, slow exhale, Herb stared for a moment at the dying doobie in his grasp and muttered, "Damn, I forgot."

Bud grinned, "It's about fuckin' time, bro!"

"Fuck it," said Herb. He fired up an EternalFlame to reignite the doobie. "I made it a month, wonder how long I'll last next time."

"I wonder why you wanna be a quitter," said Bud.

"What I wonder," Frank said, "is if your last name is McCracken, why the hell would parents name their son Phil?"

Herb laughed. "Or if your name is Joe, one must always worry about being average."

Frank said, "Yeah, average must suck. Right, Bud?"

"Fuck you," said Bud. "Want an average choke-hold applied, bitch?"

Frank smirked and pointed toward the door. "No thanks, let's cut out of here instead."

"Right on," said Bud. "She's all fueled up and ready to set sail. Get the rollup, Herb."

Bud reached down to flip a switch under his seat then pressed a chrome button on the dash panel. The motor snapped to life with an exhaust tone rumbling out the tail pipes like a gnarly Fahrvergnügen symphony.

The buggy eased away slower than a three-legged arthritic dog, and Herb rolled the door down behind. Then he made a beeline for his computer, relit the joint, and sat there puffing and pondering. In an instant, he went from zero to a hundred and got busy banging away on his keyboard. He puffed away, brainstorming and scribbling notes for several hours.

When Frank and Bud returned, Herb greeted them with an oversized smile and a cheerful update. "Without you two numbskulls hanging around bugging me, I got very creative and made a significant breakthrough."

Bud crouched down onto one knee to spin an invisible microphone stand, and then he presented the sign of the horns with pinkie and index finger while growling, "What's the Dio, Ronnie James?"

"When the parts arrive – with a power source – the Love Bus will be fully operational," Herb said. "I came up with a way to give it a power source. Then we can road test..."

Frank laughed. "Man, that's what you've been saying for months."

"Wait a second," Bud grumbled. "Let him finish."

Herb got to babbling quicker than an auctioneer on amphetamines. "Okay, so I was thinking about what I said earlier, when it suddenly occurred to me; instead of an on-demand power source, we can build an onboard generation system that keeps a battery system at maximum charge."

"How's that gonna work?" quizzed Bud.

Herb pointed to his pencil-drawn image that resembled squares drawn by Salvador Dali, and then hurried to explain before it dripped off the page. "I'll wire four 8-volt batteries in series to make a 32-volt battery – the voltage of the drive motors. There is plenty of room inside the Love Bus, so I can parallel together as many 32-volt battery packs as we need to give the motors enough available amperage to develop maximum torque."

"That sounds awesome," said Bud. "What kind of batteries?"

Herb shrugged. "Great question, dude. Not sure – I still need to look into that – but they will need an operational temperature range between 40 and 150° Fahrenheit, must accept a rapid charge, and be rechargeable hundreds of times. I'm hoping to achieve at least a 300-mile range."

Bud smiled. "That's some great news, because my buggy's 100 percent complete."

"I have even more good news," Herb said. "The parts' driver called about ten minutes ago, and the shit is on its way here as we speak."

Bud's smile widened as he pumped his fist. "Well then, let's burn one while we wait."

Half a doobie later, a box truck pulled up to the gate and the driver tooted the horn.

"I don't believe it," Herb said. "The parts are finally here. Bud, go open the gate and show the driver where to unload."

"What's the magic word?" Bud said.

Herb smiled and said, "Please."

Bud chuckled. "No, the magic word is abracadabra!"

He jogged out to open the gate, and then directed the driver as he backed toward the load-in door. Five feet shy of the door, Bud held up his hand as a stop sign.

When the driver stepped down from the cab, Herb greeted him with a quick handshake. "I can't believe you finally made it. What took you so long?"

The stone-faced driver lazily scratched his ass then shrugged. "Actually, I was on my way here at nine-thirty this morning – fueling up at the gas station right on the corner – but my boss called on the radio and ordered me to make my Orange County delivery first."

# 11

It only took Frank and Bud a week to bolt on drive motors, install gull-wing doors, and complete the wiring. Except for one minor detail, the Love Bus was a functional electric vehicle.

The minor detail being that, unable to locate batteries matching his demanding criteria, Herb decided to wait and further research the available technology before spending thousands on "shit that's just going to be temporary."

Without those batteries, it did not take Bud long to grow tired of driving the Love Bus the length of three extension cords and back. To Herb's consternation, Bud's boredom led to the launch of a new sidetrack project. Over a three-week period, Bud tinkered, smoked, tinkered, and smoked while perfecting his newest invention, which he deemed the BongRiteEndlessHigh. When triggered, Bud's BongRite blasted a steady stream of smoky sweet intoxication straight at any and all willing waste-cases, or those within dose proximity.

Even though his contraption was about as big as a refrigerator, the design was quite basic. Inside the giant metal box was a self-igniting, weed-pellet-fed water pipe connected to an air pump with hoses. The hearth-stove gave him the idea to use weed pellets, which burned evenly and fed efficiently through the device. With the simple push of a button, pellet-formed pot passed through the killer-zone firing-line where it was set ablaze. The resulting smoke got suck-filtered through a gallon of water then pulsated out the hose's other end. Thus, an instant shotgun-blast of smoke became available to anyone within the silly nozzle's reach.

Despite Herb talking major shit every time he saw anyone using one, Bud had already built and installed two BongRites in the warehouse – one in the workshop and one in the kickback area near the spot the Weeble Bong once camped, prior to retirement with nary a spill.

Frank loved the BongRite so much that he wanted one bad! Due to fueling issues and lack of free space at Frank's place, Bud was forced to build a compact unit to put a halt to the relentless pestering of, "C'mon, dude make me one."

Building the MiniBongRite was a challenge, but after several tinkering days, Bud managed to knock out a device that held one cup of pot-pellets, and then he crammed all the works into a junk microwave oven.

After staying up most of the night putting finishing touches on the new unit, when he awoke, Bud hurried to Frank's apartment to show it off.

They sat around all day watching baseball while burning almost a cup of O.G. Kush pellets. In the early evening, Herb came around searching for them and discovered those two slouched on a couch amongst scattered beer cans and empty pizza boxes. He opened a window then pointed at the MiniBongRite and spoke in a tone of righteous indignation, "I can't believe you waste all your time on that bullshit."

Bud attempted to sit up, but halfway there changed his mind and perched on an elbow to grumble, "What do you mean? You don't even have anything left for us to do, bitch."

"Actually, moron, while you were over here playing around with your little weed-wasting-machine, this morning when the batteries arrived I installed them in the Love Bus all by myself." Herb smiled and stomped his foot. "Now the vehicle will run up to forty miles."

"What batteries?" As he sat straight up, Bud's eyes opened wider than at any point during the previous hour. "Hey, wait, my Bus is on the road again?"

"Kind of," Herb said with far less zeal than a moment before. "Unfortunately, my calculations were a little off. So when I drove fifteen miles away from the warehouse, I had to have the Love Bus towed back the last two."

"How many batteries you install?" Bud said.

"I put four 32-volt battery packs in there," Herb said. "By my calculations, those batteries hold about twelve useable kilowatt hours of juice, and I'm almost positive that they had a full charge."

Bud laughed. "Wow, if it only ran that far, we're gonna need a shitload of power from those generators."

"It will be far more efficient when I finish engineering the computer code and tweak my efficiency algorithms," Herb said. "But you got so sidetracked with your idiotic project, I never got to it."

Bud took a BongRite blast, blew a few smoke rings, and smiled. "My idiotic project rules. Plus, it's done. What do you need us to do on the Love Bus, bro?"

"I could use help with more practical road tests on power loads, drag-coefficients, and system controls," Herb said.

Frank stood up, shook the tingles from his left leg, and then took some time reaching for his toes. After a head scratch and belch, he asked, "Are you gonna leave it as an electric vehicle?"

"The batteries are only temporary," Herb said, "until I settle on a cannabis conversion method."

"Cool!" Frank snuck a quick blast while Herb tech-babbled.

"Even though I am disappointed by the present lack of anything even approaching a serviceable range," Herb said, "I am very happy with the overall vehicle that I have developed. I can feel in my bones a breakthrough is imminent. But if I cannot solve this riddle within the next six months, I might very well shift my focus to extending the vehicle's battery-powered range."

While blasting an extended smoke-stream straight into Herb's face, Bud grinned like the infamous Tijuana burro performing in one of those fabled tourist shows, where the señorita seldom smiles. Save your money.

The sativa stream ceased the instant Bud lifted his finger from the trigger.

Herb, silenced by the smoke soak, showed no anger. Instead, he put on a sideways smile while mumbling, "I think I can hang out here a few minutes longer, maybe get a better idea about how Bud's device works."

Bud laughed, "Maybe if you weren't so busy constantly ragging me, you would've checked it out at home."

"I have to keep focused there." Herb examined the device a bit closer, and it wasn't too long before he figured out how to make it go and go and go.

Bud laughed, "Focused on bitch mode."

"Exactly, idiot," Herb smiled and blasted Bud.

Bud let out lungs full of smoke. "Guys, I've been thinking about something that's been bugging me a lot lately. Why do they need someone to do sign language at news conferences or concerts? Does the deaf reporting service have to send a deaf reporter to an event? I don't get it. If they can't hear, shouldn't they just read the bottom of the TV screen like old people do?"

"What?" asked a bleary-eyed Frank. "You know, buddy-boy, this thingamajiggy works way better than that fish-tank pump one you rigged up."

Herb said, "I don't remember that."

"That's because you were sleeping, man." Frank laughed and blasted him.

"That shit's as useless as the Goodyear blimp over a domed stadium," Bud said. "I've seen them do both on TV – the blimp and the sign language news."

"Deep breath, dude, deep breath," Frank said. "There are far bigger issues."

Bud scratched his head and stared at the wall for several seconds. "Like what?"

Frank wore the wicked grin of visualized vulgarity. "Okay, dude, check this one out. A few summers ago, while cruising my Harley, I spotted a bunch of scantily-clad beauties milling about outside the community college theater. Intrigued, I parked and went to scope out the delicious plethora of promising prospects. There were at least ten totally fuckable honeys there, plus my only competition was a bunch of goofy short dudes."

Herb smiled. "Now I know why you decided to go to college out of the blue."

Frank nodded. "Yup, worst part is, I was just about to bang a cutie when I found out she was only seventeen."

Herb lost his smile and raised his voice. "You should have known that high school kids go to community colleges."

"See, that's my whole point," Frank said. "They should make high school girls wear something identifying them as underage, so no one gets in trouble. The real crime is the shit those illegal chicks wear. They need to cover those little babes with a burka or something.

"Put a scale next to your bed, bro." Bud cackled. "If they don't weigh a buck, don't fuck 'em."

Herb seethed in silence while shaking his head like a father reading the disappointing report card of his nineteen-year-old high school freshman.

"I tell you, it's not fair to me," Frank whined. "If that fruit's not ripe, why is it on the fucking market?"

Herb screeched, "You're a lecher!"

"Maybe so," Frank said with a smirk and a nod. "But 'I got some bad news for you, Sunshine.' That's the way most men, and plenty of very cool women, are programmed. If God didn't want us to fuck 'em, why did He make 'em so good?"

"You mean 'Why did She?'" said Bud.

"He, She, it matters not," Herb said. "With cretins like Frank slithering around, it's even more proof that there's no God."

"I know for sure that God exists," Frank said, "because He's always fucking with me."

Bud chuckled. "Dude, if there really is a God, you're in deep shit."

"I'm mostly a good guy," Frank said. "I'm fully aware that Jesus saves. But I'm guessing it's at a different bank than me, because I've never seen him at mine."

Blasphemy always put Herb in a good mood, so he giggled. "Too funny."

"I love Christians," Bud said. "They pray for me."

Herb took a blast. "Whatever. You're a dummy."

With a quick shrug, Bud smiled. "A preacher once told me, 'Christians aren't perfect. They're just forgiven.' I asked him, 'Can Christians still smoke pot?' And he said, 'Sure they can.

But would you smoke pot in front of the Lord?' I told him, 'If Jesus is cool with wine, he'd love pot.'"

"Good point," Frank said. "Wine and weed go together like loaves and fishes."

Herb jumped up from the couch. "Fuck, I just remembered, the tow truck dropped the Love Bus in front of the warehouse. That's why I came over here." He shot toward the door. "We need to get over there and push it around back before anything happens to it."

"Shit," said Bud. "Let's get the fuck over there quick!"

About half a block shy of the warehouse, Frank slowed his car to a crawl and nudged Bud out of a daydream to point out two shadowy figures snooping about the Love Bus. "You know those guys?"

As they tooled along past the property, Bud scooted down low into his seat and peered over the sill. For some reason, he whispered, "Those are the same dudes that I saw the day my Chevy got snatched. The ones Herb thinks are cops."

"I think Herb's right," Frank said. "They for sure might be cops."

"I'd bet money they're not." Bud gestured toward the other side of the street. "Just park right there, so we can watch. Maybe they'll lead us to my Camaro."

Frank checked back over his shoulder, whipped a U-turn, and eased to a stop at the curb. "Your ride is long gone, bro."

Those words of discouragement were just past Frank's lips when Herb's car came bouncing into the lot and screeched to a halt inches shy of the Love Bus.

The startled trespassers turned tail and high-stepped it around the corner as Herb shouted expletives at their backsides.

He started after them, but the pursuit ended when Herb broke it off to answer his phone. The caller ID let him know to yell, "Where the fuck are you two idiots? I just had to..."

Herb stopped screaming, looked up the block, and calmed down. "Oh, right, that's a great idea. You do that while I charge up the Love Bus."

Frank and Bud followed the men to an industrial area not too far away, parking half a block up the street from where the men's car disappeared behind a gate.

Bud hopped from the car. "I'll go peek through the fence to see what's going on back there."

"I'll leave the motor running," Frank said.

After a brief scouting trip, Bud scampered back and spent a moment catching his breath before reporting, "They went into a bungalow. It's a half-empty lot, with like a hundred cars scattered around. Way too dark to see anything else."

"Let's go tell Herb," Frank said. "See what he wants to do."

"Sounds like a plan," Bud said. "Just a little more recon first. I think there's an alley in the back." He pointed. "Head that way so we can scope it out."

After getting the lay of the land, Frank and Bud made their way back to the warehouse. When they entered the workshop, the Love Bus' gull-wing doors were spread wide open as if about to take flight. Herb had his head under the dash and his mind in the future.

"We found out where those guys went!" Frank yelled.

Herb stepped out, diagnostic module in hand. "I forgot to factor in the weight of the batteries. That's probably why she didn't even make thirty miles."

"That sounds about right," Bud said. "Plus, once you cycle them a few times, I'd bet they'll get a better range."

"I could order enough batteries for eight more packs," Herb mused. "That will increase the range by about 200 percent."

Bud counted on his fingers. "So, almost a hundred miles?"

"You think we need more?" asked Herb.

Bud poked his head inside the Bus. "Dude, there's tons of room left in there."

"I know," Herb said. "But I only installed those batteries for road-testing purposes, and to work out all the bugs while figuring out my propulsion method."

"Right on," Bud said. "But, how soon till she's charged up? I wanna take her for a cruise."

"Best wait till morning," Herb said. "The batteries should be fully charged, and…"

"Fuck that shit," Frank roared. "Are you two forgetting about the cops creeping around?"

"Forget about those guys," Herb grumbled. "Just don't leave any cars out front, and for sure don't do any deals with anyone that we have never done business with before."

"I think Frank's right," Bud said. "If they're the ones who took my Camaro, I want to get it back."

Frank groaned, rolled his eyes, and threw his arms in the air. "I guess you aren't even worried about what would happen if those cops busted our operation."

"There's no way cops would run off like that," Herb said. "If they had any info, they'd have a warrant. So don't give them any reason to come back, and stay away from their place."

Bud grumbled, "But, bro, we got…"

Herb cut him off, "ENOUGH! I don't want you guys sidetracking on that shit. Let's stick to the Love Bus."

"Whatever." Bud turned to leave. "Let's go kick back and BongRite, bro."

"Just remember my objections when it all comes crashing down." Frank quit trying to stare a hole through Herb and headed for the kickback area.

Herb yelled behind, "I'm serious. I need your help tomorrow."

Bud hollered as he stepped through the door, "I'll be here, at least long enough to tool around in the Love Bus for a while."

After an hour's worth of BongRite blasts, Bud still could not relax and just forget about those two men. He kept hatching plans, that Frank continued poking holes through.

"I got it," Bud said. "We put a bait car out front, and when they snatch it we take 'em down and hold them for the cops."

"That's the worst idea yet," Frank scoffed. "It's got two of my least favorite elements: sitting around doing nothing and COPS!"

"Well then," Bud said, "I think this situation calls for the Plague."

"What the fuck is 'the Plague'?"

"It's top secret," Bud said. "If I tell you, I'll have to kill you."

Frank grimaced. "Dude, that joke hasn't been funny since way back in the early eighties, and then only for a few weeks, a shorter lifespan than breakdancing."

Bud gave a quick nod followed by a shrug. "Whatever, bro. Guess I better start at the beginning. So last year, me and Herb developed an extremely potent strain, so fuckin' crazy it's like a chronic plague on da' brain. That's why we called it Purple Bubonic. You don't even have to smoke it. With even the slightest touch, its super-strength THC will send you on a trip past the outer limits in search of cinnamon buns."

Frank's brow arched. "You're bullshitting me, right?"

"No way, dude." Bud popped up from the couch. "Wait a sec, I'll go grab it. You'll see!"

Bud returned clutching a small hardwood box, not much bigger than three stacked decks of playing cards, and placed it on the table. "Let me show you something wicked." He opened the box to reveal a golf-ball-sized bud more colorful than a love child produced from the furious union of a unicorn banged by a rainbow in a seedy motel's filthy bathroom.

Frank ogled the wonder-weed and just about drooled. "That shit's fucking intense."

"Yep, but that ain't the even coolest thing," Bud said. "Go turn out the lights, bro."

"Is the party over?" Frank chuckled and went to flip the switch.

The room went pitch black, except for a semi-bright, greenish-purple light emanating from the wooden stash box.

Frank howled, "Holy shit! That pot is glowing in the dark!"

Bud laughed a little mad-scientist laugh. "Eh-eh-hahhh! Yep, it's crazy-fuckin'-gnarly!"

Frank turned on the lights and then went for the wooden box. "I gotta try a hit of that shit."

Bud just about tripped over himself lurching to block his hand. "Careful, bro – you'll be sorry if you touch it. That bud right there is about nine grams but, believe it or not, has more THC than a kilo of The Chronic."

"That's impossible," Frank said.

"I shit you not," said Bud. "I only took three hits of this Plague stuff, and all I remember is lighting the second hit, writing an opera with Keef, then next thing was a couple of days later waking up at the zoo with my arm halfway up a very cute rhinoceros' ass."

Frank shook his head and bitched, "You mean you two developed a super strain of marijuana that intoxicates just by touch? Why was I not informed about that shit?"

"I wanted to," Bud said with a shrug, "but Herb told me not to. Said you'd just dose people who pissed you off."

"But wait," Frank said, "isn't that what we're going to do?"

"Exactly, so don't tell Herb." Bud gestured a zip of the lips. "It's the only way we can find out what happened to my Camaro."

"I'm cool with that." Frank nodded and smiled. "What's the plan?"

"It's pretty simple," Bud said. "All we got to do is somehow get those guys to touch this bud."

"I got a way better idea," Frank said. "I'm thinking we make some Plague pellets and head over there with the MiniBongRite to blast those guys back to the stoned-age."

Bud grinned and nodded. "It's on, bro!"

# 12

The next morning, Frank and Bud took forty-two and a half laps around the block and then pushed the Love Bus back to the shop so Herb could download the system data to *anal-ize* while the vehicle recharged.

The task kept him so focused that Herb did not realize the guys spent the rest of the day manufacturing a pile of potent Plague pellets. Normally it took Bud less than an hour to produce a pound of pellets, but the full hazmat suit slowed the process to a crawl.

By nightfall, Frank and Bud were ready to set forth on their quest for answers about the mysterious men's intentions. Their mission required night vision goggles, two-way radios, a borescope, a hundred feet of two-inch polyvinyl tubing, elbow-length rubber gloves, a quarter cup of Plague pellets, and the MiniBongRite with a capful of Pine-Sol added to the water tank as a masking agent.

The guys parked in shadows cast by mid-century street lamps, up the block from the fenced property where the previous night they had followed Thursday and Jefferson.

Bud rubbed his hands together. "Let's go over our plan one more time, bro."

"Okay," said Frank. "First, you head around back and I'll make a huge racket in front to draw them out. Then, you get up on the roof and tap into the ventilation system to feed in the camera and poly tubing."

Bud nodded. "Perfect. By the time that I've got my stuff installed, and visuals on the borescope screen, you'll be ready to hook up the other end of the tube to the BongRite."

"You give me the signal and I'll blast those bitches," Frank laughed.

"Right on." Bud opened his door and smiled. "You ready?"

Frank grinned and pumped his fist. "Let the head games begin."

Just shy of an hour later, Bud stood on the roof with eyes fixed to the video screen. He twisted the tube snaking down the vent, manipulating the camera's field of view until he had a clear shot of his targets.

The men sat at separate desks, facing one another, pouring over handwritten notes and entering data into computers. Every few seconds, Thursday retrieved the burning cigarette from his ashtray and took a couple of drags while staring off into space high above Jefferson.

With the camera in place, the air conditioning tapped into, and the BongRite connected, Bud gave the signal to fire it up.

Frank locked the trigger on full blast with a Velcro strap, and less than two minutes later, Bud's monitor showed a small brush fire's worth of smoke pouring from the ceiling vent halfway between Thursday and Jefferson.

Twelve seconds later, Thursday stopped typing and yelled in Jefferson's direction while pointing to the vent.

Bud radioed, "Shut it down, pronto, right on."

Thursday jumped up and went to the spot right below the vent, then pointed to the ceiling while waving an arm and speaking toward Jefferson. By the time Jefferson glanced up from his work, the smoke was only one man's memory. So he went back to typing while Thursday shrugged, looked up one more time, and then went back to his computer.

Three minutes later, both men lay facedown upon their desks. It did not happen gently. So after Bud radioed, "Dude, you just missed the most gnarly face plants, right on and out," they both had a quick laugh at other's expense before setting off for the rendezvous point.

Frank jumped the fence and met Bud by a side window, working to jimmy the lock.

"Got it," said Bud. He paused to point inside. "That old guy is Thursday, and the black guy is Jefferson."

"Dude, let's do this." Frank tugged at the window, attempting to slide it open.

Bud yanked the arm away. "Whoa, step back, bro. We gotta wait for smoke to clear before we can go in."

Frank backed off a few feet. "How long you think they'll be out?"

Bud held his breath, slid the window all the way up, and jumped backward. "I dunno." He shrugged. "But I forgot to mention a few interesting side effects. As soon as they shed all body hair and their nuts fall off, they might-could be zombied until the next full moon."

The blood drained from Frank's face and his ears twitched as he grabbed his package and managed to choke out, "Really?"

Bud cracked up. "Nope, just fuckin' with you, bro. They'll be out for long enough. Best you get all the gear back to the car, just in case we gotta split real quick."

"I'll be back in a flash," Frank said.

Bud turned toward row upon row of parked cars. "I'm gonna check the lot for my Camaro. Meet you back here in ten."

Ten minutes later, Bud returned, kicked at the dirt, and griped, "I didn't see it, too fuckin' dark around here."

Frank motioned toward the open window. "I got some bad news, too."

A few steps and a quick glance through the window, the bad news was obvious. Thursday and Jefferson were wide awake, carrying on a boisterous conversation.

"That's not what I heard," Jefferson said with a toothy smile. "Back at A.S.S. Academy, we had a saying …"

With eyeballs spinning in opposite directions, Thursday interrupted, "A.S.S. Academy?"

Jefferson took a deep breath, and for a while forgot to exhale, until he blurted, "You know what I'm talkin' bout, mutha-fucka!" He began giggling right straight into full-force cracking up.

Thursday lost his train of thought for a moment, until kind of sort of picking up near where he left off. "Aaa, ca-ca-caademy – call the sarge – I feel funny."

Jefferson's eyes had grown larger than B-movie flying saucers. "Good funny or bad funny?" he asked before erupting in laughter.

Thursday giggled out, "Good funny," before he too dropped in to catch a massive wave of fits and giggles.

The laughter stopped on a dime, and the men froze up like ice statues. A minute passed, yet there they remained, motionless.

Frank broke the silence. "What now?"

While Bud considered options, Thursday reanimated and began giggling like a nude school girl meeting her favorite teen idol. He began tickling Jefferson's ribs, and he too awoke to join in on teehee time.

Thursday, face suddenly devoid of friendliness, spoke in a serious, all-business tone, "I just remembered something very important. It's life or death, partner."

Jefferson's laughter ceased quicker than a new bride loses motivation for dick sucking. "What's wrong?"

With an expression grimmer than one inspired by leftover tuna casserole, Thursday turned toward the other side of the office and paused momentarily before a double-wide grin washed over his face. "We have a whole pack of Oreos over there."

Jefferson put an arm around his shoulder. "Hell yes, partner. I am the Cookie Monster from outer space; take me to your Oreos."

The men stumble-laughed shoulder-to-shoulder across the room then got busy rummaging through a cupboard above the microwave.

After their frenetic expedition ended, apparently Oreos weren't enough. Laden with snacks, they traveled the least-direct route possible by zigzagging across the room, where both men attempted to sit Indian style on the floor in front of a TV.

After several tries, and chuckling-falling-overs, Thursday's lack of flexibility had him settle on sitting straight legged while propped on an elbow. He clicked the remote control. "Let's watch TV."

Thursday mashed the channel-up button, and then sped six trips through the channel lineup before pausing to read the text plastered across the screen. *The Jerry Springer Show*'s title said: "My Plain Vanilla Girlfriend Gave Birth to a Chocolate Baby."

Jefferson snickered, "Leave it here."

"Must have went for the inches." Thursday laughed.

With a nod and grin, Jefferson said, "Probably, buddy."

Thursday gave his friend a quick elbow jab to the ribs. "Why did the black guy wear a tux to get a vasectomy?"

Jefferson tilted his head back and dialed back his smile. "Why, man?"

Thursday grinned, paused, and then said, "He told the doctor, 'If I'm gonna be impotent, I wanna look impotent!'" He sold the ancient joke with a laugh and slap on the back.

Jefferson grimaced like he had eaten a three-day-old cauliflower, broccoli, and bean burrito that was dancing a jig on his gut. With that unfriendly expression in control of his facial muscles, he barked, "Whoa, motherfucker. That shit's way out of line."

Thursday's smile remained. "Ha ha, you almost got me, buddy."

"I'm serious, asshole. Watch your shit," said Jefferson.

"You know what your problem is?" growled a no longer giddy Thursday. "You guys take everything way too serious; like we're all out to get you."

"That's because most of you are," Jefferson said.

"Truth is," Thursday said, "most of us love you guys like family."

Jefferson shook his head. "Keep telling yourself that."

"I sure wish I was black," Thursday grumbled. "That way I'd have a built-in excuse for absolutely everything."

Jefferson gave a cold, piercing stare and raised his voice a few notches. "I knew it. Typical white-trash motherfucker, that's all you are."

Enough of the happy-go-lucky shit, both men bolted up and faced off toe-to-toe.

When Jefferson stepped at him, Thursday pushed him away and roared, "I guess that would make you a stupid fucking monkey."

Jefferson yelled, "My next impression: Mike Tyson!" then he flew fists-first toward Thursday, who ducked the punch like a matador does a raging bull.

In the blink of an eye, the men reestablished positions, once again meeting face-to-face. Both spied an opening and seized the opportunity to swing from the heels, landing simultaneous haymakers squarely upon the other's glass jaw to knock one another out cold.

Outside the window, Frank rubbed his eyes and stammered for only the third time in his life. "Damn, that shit's crazy. What do we do now?"

"Let's get the fuck in there and take a quick look around before they wake up," Bud said.

Frank agreed by scampering through the open window and then reached to help Bud in.

Once Bud regained his footing, he looked to where Frank's attention was focused. High on the wall, behind the desk where Jefferson sat earlier, a flat-screen TV broadcasted video surveillance of the front of Herb's warehouse.

"Holy shit," said Bud. "No wonder these fuckers show up when we got a car out there for the first time in months."

"That sure is some fucked-up shit," said Frank.

"We'll handle that later." Bud tossed a thumb drive to Frank. "Let's copy all their documents. You get Jefferson's computer and I'll get Thursday's."

Frank pointed to the monitor and cried out, "Oh fuck, look – there's a cop at your front door."

On the monitor, in living color, a police officer was rapping his knuckles onto the glass while leaning in close enough to peer though the warehouse's front door. He waited a few seconds and then knocked again.

Frank and Bud were glued to the screen, so much so they failed to notice that Jefferson had come to. He was sitting up with his back to them, nudging Thursday.

Frank glanced over to see Thursday stirring to life and gave Bud a quick shove before diving out the window. And then Bud almost landed on him.

From behind the sill, the guys peeked back inside to see Jefferson rise to his feet. A few pounding heartbeats later, he leaned down to offer Thursday a hand up.

On his feet again, Thursday looked through the window, right at Bud, and bellowed, "Who's that, there?"

Before Thursday made it two steps toward the window, Frank and Bud were three steps toward Mexico.

# 13

After Frank and Bud's snooping mission, a week passed with no blowback, or even the slightest hint of repercussion. Then there was the cop they witnessed spying through Herb's front door. He merely left a business card – "Sergeant Stan Halen" – with "Call me A.S.A.P: VERY IMPORTANT!!!" written on the back.

So, after Frank and Bud located and disabled the surveillance camera, Herb was eager to move on and just hide his head in the sand regarding any potential dangers ahead.

The fact that nothing jail-like went down gave little comfort to Bud. He remained on high alert, refusing to step foot outside the warehouse, and so wound up that something as slight as a mouse fart made him jump out of his boots.

Herb continued his ongoing attempts at soothing the anxiety. "I keep telling you, I've researched every law enforcement agency – federal, state, and local – A.S.S. does not exist!"

Frank wasn't buying it. "They're definitely law enforcement! I heard them say, 'A.S.S. Academy,' and, 'Call the Sarge,' with my own ears."

Bud said, "And they were monitoring this building, dude."

"Let's not ignore that cop right at your front door," added Frank.

"I'll call him one of these days," Herb said. "He's probably just selling tickets to a pancake breakfast for widows and orphans or something. We're legit here."

"Look, bro," Bud said. "We're under surveillance; we need to take precautions. There's about twenty times more pot in this place than three people are allowed."

"We have all the proper paperwork," Herb said. "It's a co-op."

"We're totally fucked," said Bud.

Frank pried his attention away from the security monitors long enough for a quick nod. "We need to hook your iPad up to the network's video feed, buddy-boy."

"Great plan," said Bud. "That way I'll never miss a thing."

"You're the poster child of what happens to someone who burns an ounce of pot at a sitting," Herb said. "The imagination runs wild."

"Dude, what the fuck?" whined Bud. "You're usually way more paranoid than me."

"They were only watching the front, so we won't use that entrance again. Simple!" Herb begged, "I wish you two would just forget about your paranoia shit."

"Well, I'm gonna sleep by my escape tunnel and keep my guard up." Bud shot a BongRite blast straight at him. "I'll visit you at least once a month to put money on your books."

"Whatever, idiot," Herb said. "Let's just concentrate on the Love Bus project."

"Bro, there's absolutely nothing left to do," Bud grumbled.

Herb, so very frustrated with his research's stagnation and the guys' A.S.S. sidetrack, had given in to Bud's tempting advice about getting high early and often and killing a few beers nightly. Thanks to the BongRite, a mere split-second of temptation often led to marijuana intoxication by even the strongest-willed freelance scientist.

The explanation for Herb's newfound insatiable yearning for weed was really quite simple. For three days straight, Bud BongRite-blasted him five minutes straight while he slept. It also might help to explain why Herb hadn't crawled out of bed until noon, or started working on his Love Bus research until nighttime. But the best part of all, before heading to his workshop to grind away until the wee hours, he would often cook up a massive dinner for all.

Ever since the pre-wake and bake began, Herb had gone on and on about "having a creative burst lately." The newfound creativity had nothing to do with alternative fuels. It was more about delicious, gluttonous desserts. Baking is science, too.

Herb stood and stretched. "Anyone hungry? I think I'll go whip something up."

Bud nodded. "I could eat."

While slowly rubbing his belly, Frank smiled. "I thought you'd never ask."

Not too long after devouring a splendid feast of spinach salad with crispy bacon and drizzled balsamic-vinaigrette dressing, tender and juicy tri-tip, home fries, and crusty sourdough baguette dipped in extra-virgin olive oil, it was off to the couch for an after-dinner BongRite session.

"This project's extended timeline and cost overruns have been absolutely stunning to me," lamented Herb. "I was hoping that you two might consider investing to help get me over the finish line. Your R.O.I. could be tremendous."

Bud blasted him. "My mom's house payments get my extra dollars."

Frank flipped him off. "Fuck that shit. I'm going to buy that Vette I've had my eye on."

Herb shook his head and frowned. "You shouldn't waste all your money on a toy. Buy something more practical, and with the leftover money you can give to the poor, or help inner city kids get sports equipment; anything to give back and not be so greedy."

Frank laughed and waved off the unsolicited advice. "'Give back' implies that I took something. When you complete the Love Bus, are you going to donate your profits to mankind? Or spend large chunks of your windfall purchasing happiness' younger, cuter sister?"

Herb took a swig of beer. "The whole project is for the betterment of mankind and the planet."

Frank enjoyed an extended blast then grinned as smoke poured from his ears. "Make a choice, buddy. It's one or the other – mankind or planet!"

Herb scowled. "That's not true, and you know it."

"Well, at the rate he's going," Bud chuckled, "no need to worry about that shit anytime soon."

Herb spent a moment staring at a micro-blemish on the wall behind Bud, and then sunk down low, hung his head, and sighed, "Maybe you're right, dude. When I first conceived this project, I thought for sure I'd have some kind of tangible results by now. Six months' work, with so little to show from my experiments or the conceptual models built. It's a little depressing."

"What do you mean nothing to show?" Bud asked. "We're almost there, bro."

Herb held his head a wee bit higher while trying to smile. "I should just focus on making the Love Bus run further on batteries. Once I perfect the computer code, and tweak some of the electronics, there will be a drastic improvement of the vehicle's current seventy-mile range."

"I still think we should try getting the Love Bus running on weed," Bud said. "There's barely any space left inside for batteries. Hell, just opening and closing the gull-wings eats up 5 percent of their charge."

"I think I need a night off to do something fun for a change," Herb said.

Frank gave him a wink a grin and a blast. "What you thinking, bro – hookers and blow?"

Herb sat up straight then leaned forward and smiled. "Seeing as I'm at a complete standstill, might as well head to the Indian casino to blow off some steam. They have dollar tacos, plus two-dollar Coronas and margaritas all night long."

"Way to go, man. Cheap food and drinks combined with slutty squaws – genius!" Frank grinned. "I'll alert the cavalry if you're not back by sunrise tomorrow. We'll look for what's left of you at the 'greasy-grass.'"

"I have a great idea." Bud smiled and passed the BongRite. "How about using a weed-pellet-feeder to run some generators and power the drive wheels like that? We can play around and run some tests on a cup of pellets at a time."

Herb grimaced and tossed the BongRite aside. "There's no possible way that could ever be efficient. I thought you understood what I'm seeking, nothing less than a revolutionary breakthrough of maximum energy output while creating near-zero emissions. Lord knows I have explained that to you several thousand times. Besides, I'm leaning heavily toward making the Love Bus a purely electric vehicle."

As he sought to change Herb's mind, Bud blasted him with a steady smoke stream. "All I'm saying is, you've been wracking your brain for months and have nothing to show for your stress. You got no experiments going right now, so what's wrong with trying my idea?"

Herb could be heard from within the ever-expanding cloud. "The more you talk, the more I'm convinced that batteries are the way to go."

"I told you before we started; I still 'love the internal combustion engine.' All the work I did was for the love of weed!" Bud raised his voice and changed his tone to one who is rooting for a favorite ball player. "C'mon, man. Before you give up on OUR weed-car, at least give my pellet idea a shot." He grinned and removed his finger from the trigger. "Plus, it'll shut me up, and be a lot of fun, too, bro."

Herb stammered from within the dissipating haze. "W-well, m-m-maybe... I ma-mean..."

Frank gestured simulated masturbation and laughed. "Quit jerking his chain."

Unable to conjure up an immediate excuse, Herb threw up his arms. "Okay, seeing as you have an efficient means for producing pellets, and standardization lends itself to study, the math will be easily documented. I can show your dumb ass on paper what I already know. I will humor you by running a series of energy output, efficiency, and exhaust-composition tests. Once you see the numbers confirming your idiocy, we can fine-tune the electric Love Bus to get her range past a hundred miles."

"Right on, bro." Bud smiled and put it up for a high five.

Herb slapped him five and smirked. "You'll see!"

"Take my advice," Bud said. "Don't think you can ever have answers before the experiment."

Herb's smile faded faster than a top fuel dragster strapped to a rocket ship. "Last time I took your advice, I ended up with ten thousand bongs that I can't sell."

Frank laughed. "Exactly, brother. Just remember, when advice is offered, one must always consider the source. Just yesterday I was at the store reading a food label when a four-hundred-pound lard-ass-motherfucker waddled over and began offering me advice about diet and nutrition. I told him, 'I don't need diet advice, because ever since I started taking financial advice from the homeless I can no longer afford food – or books – so I'm only able to read labels.'"

While Bud cracked up, Herb grumbled, "You need to be more compassionate. Overweight individuals fight a never-ending battle against their weight. Believe it or not, most of those people are quite well versed on diet and nutrition. Many simply lack the time or metabolism, so they lose the will to remain fit."

"And they're still fat," Frank jeered. "So it makes sense to listen to them why? What should I do with their advice – the opposite?"

"That's the best way," Bud chuckled. "Learn from others' mistakes, so you don't feel the pain."

Herb took a quick blast and then sprang to his feet and smiled. "I'm bored; think I'll hit that casino. Bud, we will run experiments on those pellets first thing tomorrow, promise."

"That's cool, bro," Bud said. "I was just gonna lay low tonight anyways. I'll knock that shit out, and you can check it when you get up."

"Alright, sounds like a plan," Herb said. "Set it up on the far end of my workbench, near the rollup."

With thumb in the air and a bleary-eyed smile, Bud said, "Right on, bro."

Ten minutes after Frank and Herb hit the road, Bud sat at Herb's workbench visually sizing up the area while scribbling an occasional note onto a legal pad.

He mumbled, "I better bolt that puppy down, so Herb don't fuck it up."

A short time later, Bud set the pencil down and announced to the rodents and insects, "There, that ought to do it."

Bud got busy, and within forty minutes the device was secured to the workbench tighter than the James Brown band. He took a step back to admire his handiwork, and then dialed back his smile to almost zero. "Fuck, I need to rig up a steady pellet supply."

He fetched a roll of two-inch polyvinyl tubing, and after a fair amount of BongRiteing and tinkering for another few hours, he smiled and proclaimed, "Finally, all done."

Bud began cleaning up the work area, but once again halted to frown and grumble, "Dammit, it needs a counter so Herb can do his calculations."

It only took him about an hour and a half to install the counting device. Then Bud tested it by manually scooping pellets from within the hopper and allowing it to automatically reload. After repeating the process four more times, the counter read: 00005.

After a smile of jubilation and sixteen jumping jacks, he said, "Right on, good to go!"

Bud reset the counter to zero, replaced the five cups of pellets to the main hopper, and then finished the cleanup.

# 14

Two more weeks soared into the past, during which time no one saw neither hide nor hair of those A.S.S. men, nor figured out what the fuck they were up to. After Bud installed security monitors in the workshop and his bedroom, he appeared to be over the fear and back to his chill, happy-go-lucky self.

An amazing thing happened during those two weeks – Herb had not spent even a minute on the Love Bus project. While at the Indian casino, he discovered a far more appealing outlet for his creative juices, in the person of a cute and sweet hippie girl treat. Since their early-morning meeting and subsequent torrid tryst, he had spent all of his time at her place getting stoned, drinking champagne, and tripping on mushrooms.

When his new lady friend left town on business, Herb spent the night at the warehouse for a change. He was not even two steps through the door when Bud unloaded, giving him tons of grief for not running any tests on the pot pellets as promised.

Herb awoke at the crack of dawn and got right to work so that Bud would "shut the fuck up."

Herb ran tests all day, into the early evening. Surprise-surprise, Bud's idea worked better than anyone could have ever imagined, and Herb nearly came in his shorts. In Bud's infinite search to simplify the consumption of cannabis products, he stumbled upon an ultra-efficient way of unleashing the potential energy stored within marijuana's molecular structure.

After his long day of research, Herb stepped out to grab some chow. When he returned with a pizza pie, he found Frank and Bud chilling in the workshop, listening to the radio and keeping an eye on the security monitors.

Herb was full of cheer. "All right, you guys made it back."

Bud eyed the box. "Did you get enough pizza for three, bro?"

"Always." Herb happy-smiled, set the box down, and then pulled up a chair right next to them.

The guys dove for free pizza as Herb gazed to his workbench. "I cannot believe Bud's dumb idea – combined with my technological designs and utilization of proprietary super-conductivity circuits – led to my truly groundbreaking propulsion discovery."

Bud pointed at the MiniBongRite on the workbench. "I noticed it was empty, so I reloaded the pellet supply. In case you need to run some more tests."

"Thanks, but I'm done." Like an emoji stuck on stupid, Herb couldn't stop smiling. "I ran tests nonstop for twelve hours, and the numbers only got better. How many cups... did you say... that thing holds?" His voice trailed off as his head tilted down. With eyes locked onto his phone reading a text, he smirked as his thumbs got busy.

"The hopper holds exactly one cup per reload," Bud said.

Herb almost looked up while mumbling, "A cup means nothing to me."

"Sure it does." Bud waggled a finger. "Because I designed those pellets to weigh an ounce per cup, that way I'd know how much to sell them for if my BongRite ever took off."

Herb stopped thumbing his phone and looked Bud straight in the eye, but did not utter a word.

There they all sat in silence, until Frank begged, "C'mon, dude, tell us what you found already."

"Hold up for a sec, I want to make sure." Herb shot to his feet and almost skipped his way to the workbench. After going over his notes while punching the calculator keys several dozen times and making a few quick scribbles, he turned back toward the guys with a smile spread clean across his mug. "It's even better than I thought; nothing less than miraculous, I tell you."

Herb looked past the guys and spoke to no one in particular. "It seems that whenever I am con…"

"Spit it out you, wordy fuck," Bud demanded.

Herb snapped back to the present and headed across the room to personally deliver the numbers. "It works out to a thousand miles per ounce."

Bud appeared more stupefied than usual. "Wow, bro."

Like a cat fighting to stay out of a toilet, Herbs arms and legs flew about in all directions. "Even more exciting – for that kind of energy output – the particulates, ozone, co2, hydrocarbons, or any other exhaust pollutants are mind-bogglingly low."

"You're the man!" Frank reached up to hit him with a high five. "A thousand MPOZ, that's fucking awesome, bro!"

"Well, Bud does deserve a little credit," Herb said. "For his pestering."

Bud stopped counting on his fingers and smiled. "Right on, thanks."

Herb's chest puffed out like a robin ready to rock. "Apparently, dropping out of my Ph.D. program wasn't such a huge mistake after all. Why bust my ass to become a doctor of philosophy when I'm a doer in reality? Boys, I will be remembered forever for this!"

Bud shrugged. "You think, bro?"

Herb nodded, then took a seat and reached for the BongRite. "Numbers don't lie, dude. What is the cost per ounce to produce those pellets?"

"When I crunched the numbers," Bud said, "from clone to hopper it penciled out at sixty-two bucks a cup."

Frank just about yelled, "So you're saying the Love Bus will be able to drive a thousand miles with just sixty dollars' worth of fuel?"

"My calculations could be off as much as 20 percent," Herb said. "But these numbers are still groundbreaking and planet-saving. Even when factoring in the margin of error, we are realistically speaking of a range between eight- and twelve-hundred-miles per ounce. But we can't know for sure until we install a full-scale pellet-feeder system and combine it with my computer-controlled efficiency interface."

Like a trucker with Tourette's, Bud blurted, "Shit-fuck, that's fuckin' awesome. You're saying we're gonna throw a fuckin' pellet-feeder system in my fuckin' Bus, right?"

"Whenever you're ready, dude." Herb let his thoughts drift off to a place where pride, wonder, and lots of naked ladies reside. "Just think of all the high-quality and environmentally friendly jobs we will create right here in America."

Frank smirked, "Sounds expensive, man."

Bud squirmed and hopped around in his seat like a toddler about to soil their Huggies. "What's the plan now, bro?"

"That all depends," said Herb. "How long will it take you to build a pellet-feeder device with a hundred times the BTU output of that one on my bench, rig it to run the on-demand power plant, install it into the Love Bus, and get the bugs out?"

Bud went for a notepad and spent a few minutes jotting down a work list while Frank and Herb BongRite-blasted each other six exits past the silly stage.

Bud sat at Herb's workbench, going over his plans, scratching his head, and once a minute or so adding another task to the list. He turned his head halfway to yell over his shoulder, "I think I got it."

Herb asked, "So, what's the timeline, dude?"

Bud strutted back to his seat, looking prouder than peacock in a zoot suit. "No doubt, Frank and me can knock that shit out in two weeks. Three weeks tops, bro."

"Are you sure?" Herb grinned. "Don't you guys have a dune buggy or bong lighter to build, or some other sidetrack?"

Bud patted him on the back. "Nope, already got a kick-ass buggy; and we installed all the hard stuff on the Love Bus ages ago. I guarantee you we can build the pellet-feeder, pull all them batteries out of there, and have generators powering electric motors in three weeks or less. No problem at all."

"Then I will only need two days to load software code and do final road testing to dial it all in." Herb cracked open a brew. "I think we should plan an awesome spectacle for our unveiling. We need to cap off this bitch in style!"

Frank grinned from ear to ear. "How about a casino night? We'll recreate the Bellagio fountains, and then you can get shitfaced drunk and piss in them."

Herb laughed free and easy. "Nah, I have an even better idea. We should have the unveiling on April 22."

"Why the hell do you want to celebrate Vladimir Lenin's birthday?" asked Frank.

"It's Earth Day, dude," Herb said, and then waited for Bud's two cents.

Bud took a blast and exhaled slower than two amputees running a three-legged race, smiled, and nodded. "Late April leaves plenty of time for Frank and me to fine-tune the Love Bus for her coming-out party."

"Well then," Herb said, "Earth Day it is!"

"Right on," Bud said with a pump of his fist. "Can I fire off my cannon?"

Herb grimaced like a newborn in need of a burp. "Absolutely not. Last time you did that shit, the cops swarmed the neighborhood."

Bud shrugged and smiled. "But it's a party. So it's all good, bro."

Herb shook his head and held his ground. "I still don't think it's a very good idea."

Frank nodded in agreement and Bud sulked, staring at the guys for being such buzzkills until the BongRite made him forget his... well, mostly everything.

"With more than a month to get ready, we can promote the shit out of this puppy." Frank sat on the edge of his seat. "We'll set up a website and invite representatives from major corporations, venture capitalists, the press, plus all our friends. We'll get a massive turnout if we do it right."

"I just thought of something." Bud pointed at the Love Bus. "Seeing as it's a vehicle, it doesn't make sense to just leave it parked out back. To really show her off, we gotta drive her around."

"That's a great idea," Herb said with a knee slap followed by a blast. "We will take our show on the road, with the Love Bus symbolically leading a parade of other alternative-fuel vehicles. It will signal the dawn of a new age, with no more filthy gasoline engines choking our planet with deadly exhaust."

"Great idea," said Frank. "We'll all rally here, and they can follow us on a tour of the San Fernando Valley."

Bud rubbed his belly and burped up some smoke. "Let's end up at a big cookout."

"I love it," Herb said. "Let's do it!"

With a nudge to Herb's ribs, Frank grinned like a hungry pit bull over a basket full of kittens. "Remember our first alternative-energy experiments in high school?"

Herb pondered for a moment and then shrugged. "I don't remember doing alternative-fuel experiments in high school."

Frank chuckled. "Dude, you got to remember lighting farts in the paint booth during shop class."

"Oh yeah." Herb laughed. "I sure miss those high school days."

"I hated school," Bud moaned. "Instead of teaching me shit, they always tried to control me. Yelling stuff like, 'You kids quit running in the hall!' But then they'd get mad at me for not running during PE class. I don't get it."

Frank nodded. "You know what I hated most? The boring textbooks they forced us to read. Trying to appease so many groups made those factually incorrect texts unreadable. But there were loads of chicks there, so I went."

Bud held up both middle fingers. "I always thought having to be apologetic for us winning the game of history sucked."

"Education is structure," Herb said. "My life's structure helps me improve and excel."

That got big laughs, so Herb sulked until Bud remedied it by blasting him.

Frank spoke with a twinge of anger in his voice, "What about all that 'Curiosity killed the cat' bullshit? They tried selling me that crap, but I'd ask the grownups, 'What, when, where, why, how did the lil' pussycat die?' Teachers got mad at me, said I was 'being difficult.' I was just trying to learn, brother." He shook his head. "Just trying to learn."

"Yeah, like Curious George," Bud grumbled. "Instead of encouraging kids to be inquisitive, he's always getting into trouble by checking shit out."

"Curiosity does get kids into trouble," Herb said. "For example, matches are dangerous. We don't want kids getting curious about them and then burning down the house. Do we?"

"Playing with matches is super fun!" Frank grinned. "How are you ever going to learn about fire unless you play with it?"

"I remember they tried to get us kids to stop making fun of each other and report bullies." Bud rocked back and forth and got into some serious arm flailing. "That shit don't work. Them little fuckers need to learn to laugh with the jokers and beat the living shit out of the bullies."

Frank nodded, and then did jazz hands high above his head as he sang out, "Hallelujah, brother!"

# 15

Frank and Bud welded, wrenched, and wired while Herb organized an unveiling event they dubbed "Pot as Renewable Energy," P.A.R.E. for short. With the party plans complete, invitations were sent out far and wide across the land. The R.S.V.P.s soon came rolling in, with an overwhelming number of positive responses from alternative and mainstream press outlets, as well as several entities seeking investment information.

The guys were stoked while they smoked, because they knew once the money people witnessed firsthand the Love Bus perform as advertised, Herb would be in the catbird's seat and enjoy the luxury of choosing the most lucrative offer that made the most business and ecological sense.

Frank and Bud had worked night and day for almost a month, and with four days to spare, they completed all mechanical work. All that remained was for Herb to load the software onto the vehicle's computer, and then the Love Bus would be ready for her final pot-powered road tests.

To thwart hackers' attempts at stealing his proprietary code or deliver a virus, Herb configured the Love Bus' computer software interface via two 5 ¼ floppy discs. The week before Herb needed them, while gathering up some old junk to donate to the Salvation Navy, Bud stumbled upon the box with the floppy drives and away those drives went with the rest of the unwanted crap.

Herb went apoplectic. The Love Bus showcase was days away, with no way to fine-tune the vehicle until replacements were secured.

Bud attempted to calm the situation by pointing out that they still had lots of time, and the most important ingredient – the software. He claimed that it would be "no problem to get a few drives off of Craigslist."

To prove his point, Bud got busy online shopping. Within an hour, he was at a Starbucks parking lot with a snub-nose revolver jammed into his ribs while being robbed by some dude that he met on Craigslist.

With personal safety concerns brought crying and begging to the forefront, they crossed Craig off their list and turned to eBay for solutions. To no one's surprise, there were hundreds of options to purchase obsolete crap at a fair price. So with the click of a mouse, and paying of a pal, the very next business day a package containing two 5 ¼ floppy disc drives arrived at the warehouse.

His initial joy faded quicker than a spray tan in a monsoon when Herb discovered one of the drives inoperable. Lacking enough time to order another, he spent several hours attempting to refurbish it. But it was trashed.

Herb summoned the guys to the workshop and broke the devastating news. "Unless we find another drive by tomorrow afternoon, I'm totally screwed." He leaned forward, rested forehead on arm, and whined, "I should have ordered five of these fuckers all at the same time."

Bud rubbed his shoulder. "Bro, we got this."

Frank picked up the inoperable drive, gave it a quick once over, and then tossed it back onto the bench. "I can't believe your tweaker cousin doesn't have one amongst his piles of ancient electronic junk."

Herb's cousin, Dick, owned a good-sized electronics salvage shop in Nevada. Herb apparently spaced on checking with him, because the suggestion was barely past Frank's lips when Herb began sending spittle into his phone: "Hey, Cuz. It's Herb. You wouldn't happen to have any 5 ¼ inch floppy drives lying around, would you?"

Herb looked up and arched a brow. "He's checking."

"I told ya, bro" Bud said. "'Everything will work if you let it.'"

"Meatloaf, again?" asked Frank, which caused him and Bud to crack up and start rough-housing.

Herb scowled and held up a hand.

A minute later, he broke the silence. "Yeah, I'm here."

A few more tense moments went by, but then a smile spread across his face. "That's fantastic. Okay, I'll send Frank. He'll be there in four hours."

With everyone all smiles, Bud reached out to high five Herb, only to be met by a cold shoulder.

Herb jumped to his feet. "Frank, you ready to break your record time to Vegas? Dick's leaving for a fishing trip at six in the morning, and will not wait around for you."

Frank was already halfway to the door. "I rode my Harley over. I'll jet home and grab 'the Beast' and hit the road right away, buddy."

"Wait," said Bud, "I'll go with you."

"No fucking way," Herb screeched. "I don't want to chance you fucking anymore shit up."

"I guess you're right. I'll just hang out here, and for sure fuck shit up with the Louisville Slugger." With a wicked smile, Bud called his shot then swung for the fences.

"Watch it, you son of a bitch!" Herb bellowed.

Frank smirked. "A son of a bitch is just a puppy."

"Well, I guess some ear scratching is in order." Bud nuzzled up, grinned, and yipped. "Woof woof, bro."

Herb pushed him away and gave a beady-eyed stare while clenching hands to fists a few times before stomping out without a word.

"I sure could use a joint roller." Frank jogged toward the door. "I'll be back in a flash to grab you."

Twenty minutes later, Frank's Corvette screeched into the parking lot. He laid heavy on the horn and flipped the bird to the surveillance camera, signaling Bud that it was time to hit the road to Fabulous Las Vegas.

# 16

About five hours later, aboard Raoul and Duke's ancient hippie bus slow-rolling its way through the Las Vegas resort corridor, Frank let out a long steady stream of smoke. "That's why I had to ditch the CHP."

"So you see," Bud said as he reached for what little remained of the doobie, "if we don't have at least one working disc drive back in L.A. by tonight, all that fuckin' work will be for nothing."

Raoul was digging that lovely hydro bud; really digging it! "You say you guys grow this stuff, huh?" His smile grew as he rolled the roach in his fingertips while mumbling, "Very nice."

"Yep, we got more weed than you'll ever need." Bud gave a wink and a nod. "You two get the 'friends and family discount,' too. That's about one-third retail."

Duke looked up into his rearview. "Far out, we'll for sure take you up on that."

Bud gave him a thumbs-up then checked the time on his phone. "We're only about twenty minutes away; should make it there with almost an hour to spare."

"I guess that means no one will argue if I spark another doobie." Frank lit that shit up.

He was correct. No one argued.

As the bus refilled with second-, third-, and fourth-hand smoke, Bud wondered aloud, "Why are there commercials on cable television? I thought that the ads are what pay for the shows. So how come they charge for the cable, and there are just as many fuckin' commercials?"

Raoul pointed out a capitalism truism, "They charge because people are willing to pay."

"Invest in a DVR and fast forward that shit," Frank said.

Bud grumbled, "What we really need are TV commercials that teach people how to drive."

"Yeah, right." Frank smirked. "Who's going to pay for that shit?"

"The TV stations." Bud threw his arms in the air. "They're public airwaves."

"That won't ever happen." Frank laughed and nudged him in the ribs. "Unless some concerned citizen, like you, foots the bill."

"Everyone needs to know the left lane is for passing." Bud had worked himself up to almost hot and bothered. "How hard would that be to teach the people?"

Frank put a hand on his shoulder. "Calm down and take a deep breath, man." He waved his free arm. "Think of the big picture, brother. The real question is: Why aren't TV stations responsible for stuff advertised on their airwaves?"

With a robust shake of the head, Bud disagreed. "Teaching idiots the rules of the road is much more important."

"I don't think so," said Frank. "Every day, some crook purchases TV airtime to make outrageous claims, promising folks 'money back if not 100 percent delighted.' But what happens if the product is defective, or ineffective, and the company disappears?"

Bud looked right straight through him to ponder for a moment, and then shrugged. "Who fuckin' cares?"

"Okay, let's say a person bought some penis-enlargement pills from a TV ad, and tried them for thirty days, but noticed little measurable improvement of the ol' shrinky dink." Frank chuckled. "What would you do then, Bud?"

"Ha ha, I'd tie it in a bow, bitch." Bud grinned and then punched Frank in the arm as the old guys chuckled at the nonsense.

"I'm totally serious," said Frank. "What if there's some fly-by-night operation pushing stuff like diet pills, exercise equipment, or even investments. Wouldn't it be much easier to require the station to make sure a company is a viable entity before allowing them to advertise, or make stations compensate their victims?"

Bud groaned and rolled his eyes. "Look, too bad if you can't figure out the simple fuckin' concept of never buying anything – ever – from TV or someone who calls on the phone."

Frank nearly begged, "Just think about it for a second. In reality, aren't they both partners in a conspiracy to defraud?"

Raoul added his two cents, "Frank's absolutely correct, they should make laws that truly protect consumers. The corporations stole the public airwaves from the people, and ought to be kept in check through aggressive regulation and oversight."

"I quit reading the Constitution at the 'Congress shall make no law' part." Bud reasoned, "It's gotta be way cheaper to educate than regulate. Teach people to think on their own, and maybe then they won't be such fuckin' sheep."

Duke checked the mirror then reached over his shoulder to intercept the joint. "I also agree with Frank. It would be a positive use of the public airwaves. Good Karma."

Frank looked him in the eye and scoffed, "There's no such thing as Karma."

Duke shook his head. "Oh dear, you poor child."

"Karma reveals itself to everyone at its own pace," said Raoul.

Frank smiled and shrugged and said, "Whatever."

Bud leaned forward across the railing and pointed up toward the approaching road sign. "Take a right at the next off-ramp."

After exiting the highway, and a few left and right turns, Bud stood, got in a quick stretch, and then gestured. "It's that big purple building on the right, half a block up."

"Far out, man," Duke said then slowed way down.

About a minute and fourteen-and-a-half car lengths later, Bud pointed. "Right on, just park it right here."

Wearing his hippy-go-lucky smile, Duke resembled an old dog with some fine young lass rubbing its belly. "It's all good," he said and checked his mirrors four times before easing the bus over to the curb.

Raoul pointed to his watch dial and boasted, "Told you guys we'd make it in time."

"We never doubted you." Bud passed Raoul a fresh doobie. "This should keep you guys entertained."

Raoul received the handoff like a fullback ready to charge over right tackle, nodded, and agreed, "Indeed it shall."

The instant Duke yanked on the lever opening the double glass doors, Frank bolted from the bus and yelled, "Last one there is a fag."

Bud hollered from the bottom step, "What, fags run from busses?" He looked back over his shoulder and told the old guys, "Me and the fag will be right back."

Raoul lit the bomber and took a puff. "No hurries, no worries."

Bud enjoyed a casual stroll across the parking lot. When he arrived to Frank's side, a sign hanging inside the front door rudely greeted him: "Closed: Gone Fishing."

Frank yanked and shook the door, which wouldn't budge. He reported the obvious. "It's fucking locked, dude."

Bud moved him aside, shielded his eyes, and then leaned into the glass for a better look inside. With the other hand, he made a God-awful racket, incessantly clanking a metal key ring onto the tempered glass.

While Bud clanked away, Frank walked off and disappeared around the side of the building. Not even a minute later, he returned, face flush with anger as he bitched, "His fucking boat and truck are gone."

Bud ceased the awful racket and dug his phone out. "I better call Herb to see what he wants us to do."

"This is total bullshit, man!" Frank gave a swift kick that rattled the door.

"Hey fucker, be cool," Bud barked.

Not even ten seconds later, Bud frowned and hung up. "Herb's not answering."

After three more unanswered calls, Bud left a yelled message, "Your dick cousin split before we got here. Thought you said we had till six. Call me back – NOW!"

"Motherfucker's still asleep." Frank punched the wall, then grimaced and rubbed his knuckles. "What should we do?"

Bud shook his phone. "We'll wait for Herb to call us. Maybe Dick will come back; might just be gassing up his truck."

Frank was going a hundred miles an hour, pacing in place. "And if not, then what?"

Bud placed a hand on his shoulder. "Stay positive, bro."

Ten minutes passed, and twelve more voicemails to Herb with no luck. Bud started toward the bus. "Wait here, I need to get something."

Frank yelled at his backside, "Can't you even make it twenty minutes without a smoke?"

Bud was on and off the bus in less than two minutes, and then it puttered away before he got back to Frank.

Frank tracked the bus as it disappeared from sight. "Where the hell are the hippies going?"

"They're waiting around the corner." Bud held up a crowbar and grinned. "I think we need to go on a mission."

Frank checked left, right, up, down, and all around for prying eyes. "Right on; what's the plan, bitch?"

Bud motioned toward the street. "Just stay here and keep a look out."

"I can do that!" Frank moved into position then stood with arms crossed and back to the door, scanning the scene before him.

Bud sprinted to the fence, chucked the crowbar over it, and then followed right behind.

Ninety-six seconds later, he let Frank through the front entrance.

Frank laughed, scurried inside, and pulled the door closed. "You missed your calling, buddy-boy."

Bud shrugged, nodded, and then looked toward the street. "Let me know if you see any trouble coming."

"Just hurry up and find those damn drives so we can get the fuck out of this place," Frank said before turning his focus outward.

In the back room, just past the lobby, Bud discovered that Herb's cousin was far more of a hoarder than anyone had imagined. Huge piles of every imaginable electronic part and gizmo were scattered here and there, waiting to be torn apart and inventoried before getting tossed into a bin or piled onto one of hundreds of shelves.

Five minutes later, Bud remained frozen and overwhelmed, trying to figure out where the most likely place the drives would be so he could start a search.

He began turning in slow circles while looking high and low for even the slightest hint of where they might be stored. He muttered over and over, "If I was a floppy disc drive, where would I be? If I was a floppy…"

Frank's bellowing interrupted the search process. "FUCK-SHIT-SHIT-SHIT-FUCK, COPS!"

Bud bolted like greased lightning to Frank's side, and the two stood barely hidden behind the jam.

As they peeked out, Frank whispered, "Think we can make it out the back?"

"For sure," Bud murmured. "But there's no fuckin' escape route back there."

"Well then, you better think of something quick." Frank pointed. "'The sheriff's near.'"

A few short yards across the parking lot, a police cruiser sat askew at the curb. A muscle-bound cop hurried from behind the wheel and came around the front of the vehicle, all the while moving slow and steady toward the guys and scanning the property for signs of crime.

A tall, smoking-hot, hard-bodied female officer with hair wound in Princess Leia buns stepped from the passenger side and kept pace several feet behind him.

Bud let out a heaving sigh, then whispered, "That cop is perfect."

"I don't know." Frank held his hand level, about shoulder high. "He's kind of short."

"Bro, I'm talkin' bout that fine-ass chick cop."

"I know." Frank grinned and shook his head slowly while muttering, "Lord have mercy. That shit's way too good to be true." He rubbed his crotch. "Sure would be quite a gift for a cock that has everything!"

Bud, hypnotized into a stupor by a life-long fantasy inching toward him, stepped closer to the door for a clear look.

Both officers halted in their tracks while placing a hand on their gun's butt.

The lead man bellowed toward the door, "You there. Step outside, slowly."

With his consciousness locked on the officer at the rear, and wishing that he could see it, Bud did not respond.

"Bud! Bud! Dude, he saw you," Frank said.

Bud shrugged, smiled, and pushed the door open and took a stroll toward the officers as Frank followed.

They approached the policeman, who wore a scowl upon his chiseled face and a nametag that read: "WUCEY."

Bud stopped a few feet shy of Wucey and looked past him to deliver a flirty smile to the female. "Good morning, officer. How may I help you?"

The officer stroked his mustache with his left hand then spoke forcefully. "Boy, we got a burglary alarm at this address."

Bud kept his smile, but shifted focus to officer Wucey. "It's all a big misunderstanding, sir…"

Wucey silenced him by holding up a hand. "All in good time, son. First I need some identification."

Frank and Bud passed their licenses to the officer, who took a quick glance before giving the guys a once-over. "You two are a long way from California."

"We drove out to pick up some electronic parts from our friend before he goes fishing," Bud said.

After Wucey handed back the IDs, he pointed at the curb in front of the patrol car and barked, "Take a seat while I sort things out."

He turned to his partner. "Officer Beaver, keep an eye on these two while I locate the property owner."

As Bud sat imagining Beaver fully exposed, she caught his drift and gave an impish smile. They locked gazes for almost meaningful eye contact, until she broke the rhythm and averted her eyes toward the building's entrance.

Always on the prowl, Frank tried a different approach. He painted his face with sunshine and spoke low, warm, and smooth like a late-night FM disc jockey, "You know, babe, your partner never searched us. I think for everyone's safety, you might want to perform a thorough search for weapons or contraband."

His asinine smirk was met by Bud mumbling from between clenched teeth, "Dude, I got that fuckin' sack of Bubonic."

Officer Beaver grinned like a wicked schoolgirl playing truth or dare, hoping for a naughty dare involving her best friend's stepfather. She pointed at Bud and commanded, "You, get over here and put your hands on the hood!"

Bud stood and managed to stealthily reposition his wood before shuffling sideways toward the patrol car. Then, without prompting, like an old pro, he bent forward and placed his palms down as wide across the hood as he could reach.

While using a foot to emphasize the desired outcome, Beaver barked, "Spread 'em!"

As soon as Bud complied, she began frisking him slower than honey drips during an Arctic winter. Every few seconds, Bud shuddered as Beaver patted along. Down his right leg, then up the other before slowing the pace even further right about his upper left thigh.

He hangs it on the left, so a muffled "Oh shit" escaped from Bud's lips.

"Come again?" Beaver cooed sweeter than a cherished love song from the recent, distant past. "Oh, just relax, sugar."

Of all the things that Bud could, would, or wanted to do at that particular moment in time, relaxing was not on his list.

He went into tension overload when the frisk arrived to his cargo pants pocket, and Beaver reached in to grab his sack.

She sounded almost playful. "What do we have here?"

While examining the baggy's contents, Officer Beaver smiled like an exotic dancer drowning in a wheelbarrow's worth of singles, and then offered a glowing compliment, "Oh, that's very nice!"

"It's all yours if you want." Bud smiled and winked. "I won't say a thing, promise."

She shrugged and looked toward the building. "I'm tempted, sweetie, but it's not worth my job."

Bud stood up straight and turned to face her. "You sure? Maybe if you just take a quick whiff – you'd realize that's the best stuff you've ever seen."

The lovely officer took a quick look both ways, opened the Ziploc, and then stuck her dainty nose deep inside to enjoy an immense whiff of wonder weed. A smile more stunning than a tropical sunset spread across Beaver's face.

Bud put on his best "I love you" smile and suggested, "Just hold a bud up to the light, the colors will amaze you."

Once again her eyes darted toward the door. Satisfied that the coast was clear, she removed a colossal bud to inspect by the dawn's early light, while marveling, "Wow, it's like a deep-purple diamond mine."

Bud attempted to sound suave and charming as he memorized her most excellent tits, but the words came out as a pervy mumble. "Indeed, that's some special stuff. I was hoping that you need it as bad as I want to give it to you."

Beaver clutched the buku bud in her lovely left hand and took another quick look toward the building, then winked. "Okay, sweetie, back with your friend."

Bud let out a heavy sigh then stared straight into her eyes, smiling with the goo-goo-faced look of a love-struck fool. "So we're all good?"

She smiled, checked one last time for witnesses, and nodded.

But just as she opened the baggie to stuff the bud back inside, a shit storm went off behind her eyeballs, causing them to spin like a twister in a thimble. With her consciousness possessed by horticulture heroics, a detoured Beaver laid the bud down next to the baggie on the hood and set forth on a mission of extreme importance within the car.

Bud went and took a seat back on the curb. "Fuck, almost worked."

"No biggie," said Frank. "That dick cop will have to pick up the bud. We'll make our break then."

It turned out the goal of Beaver's urgent quest was a pack of Donettes. She ripped them open with her perfect teeth and then popped the tiny tasty treat into her mouth. A look of honey-kissed bliss engulfed her angelic face.

Not even a minute later, Wucey returned to find Beaver eating Donettes. He appeared more than a little peeved by his partner's casual attitude. Until, hot damn, Beaver shot him the most agonizingly sultry smile ever, causing him to get lost in dreams and dirty desire.

The instant that he noticed the humongous colorful bud on the car's hood, Wucey snapped back to the real world and reverted to default us-versus-them mode. "Which one of those two belongs to the drugs?"

Beaver wiped powdered sugar from her pouty lips then pointed to Frank and smiled at Bud.

Wucey gave the evidence a quick once over and a sniff before returning it to the Ziploc. He pointed at Frank, waved an arm toward the patrol car, and used his megaphone voice. "Get up and put your hands on the car! I'll bet you've done this a hundred times, punk."

Frank didn't budge an inch. Instead, he waited for signs of mental meltdown.

An angered Wucey took an aggressive step forward. But Frank just smiled and spoke in a familiar, friendly tone. "It's only weed, buddy. I've got a medical card."

"You're in my state, son," Wucey roared. "Get up now!"

Frank rose and began making his way toward the cruiser, while keeping the conversation casual, "What's your trip, cop? Did some long-haired dude cornhole your daughter or something?"

Wucey's brow furrowed and his face burned crimson as he took a massive pull of air deep into his lungs. But instead of blowing up, he smiled wider than a circus clown's painted-on glee and began giggle-laughing.

Frank turned to Bud and gave double thumbs-up.

Half a minute later, with happy tears streaming down his cheeks, and near breathless from jocularity, Wucey turned toward his partner kicking back in the cruiser. "Did you eat all those donuts, Barbie?"

Frank went to sit back down. The guys waited a few more minutes, until it became quite obvious the Plague was doing its righteous boogie-woogie on cop brains.

"Grab that weed and head for the bus." Bud stood and pointed to the northeast. "I told Duke to park just around the corner."

Frank hopped to his feet and grinned. "Let's get them back for fucking with us. We'll take their uniforms home with us. I'll get hers."

Bud shot down the prank. "It's not their fault we were breaking and entering."

Frank took a quick gander at Beaver sprawled and passed out cold on the passenger seat and grumbled, "Whatever. But only because I want to get the fuck out of here."

"Can't leave that cop up there like that." Bud looked toward the naked Wucey swinging like Tarzan twenty feet above the ground on a nearby tree branch and chuckled. "You head back to L.A. to find out what the fuck happened to Herb, and I'll catch up later."

# 17

Six hours later, inside Herb's workshop, Frank finished up his reporting of events. "So, Bud stayed there to keep looking for the drives, and the hippies drove me back to Primm. Why didn't you answer your damn phone?"

Herb wore the meager grin of a pussy-whipped fool and gave a slight shrug. "I was with Kat."

Frank's eyelid twitched as he drew a deep breath. A long, slow exhale left him calm, cool, and collected while he offered the suggestion, "You need to check your messages, especially when you got friends doing important shit for you."

Herb brushed it off with the classic tactic of redirection. "I will, but right now we need to figure out what to do about the parade." He picked up a pen, jotted a number one at the top of the legal pad, and there Herb remained for several minutes, frozen, pen at the ready, eyes locked on Love Bus schematics, pondering options that jealously refused to reveal themselves.

All the while, Frank paced tight circles. After several minutes' worth of a hole worn into the concrete floor, he came to an abrupt stop and threw his arms in the air. "We're fucked, man."

Herb looked up, nodded, and slammed his pen down. "It certainly does appear so."

"Guess we should have waited till the Love Bus was running before inviting all those movers and shakers," Frank muttered.

Herb tried staring a beady-eyed hole straight through Frank's heart. Unable to shoot lightning bolts from his eyeballs, he went with screaming, "I knew you two would fuck it up somehow!"

With the gloves off, the shouting games began. Frank blew his top. "Dude, it was your cousin that fucked us. We got there with almost a fucking hour to spare."

"Sure you did," Herb bellowed. "Dick wouldn't do that. But either way, must I remind you who tossed my drives?"

Frank got one last shout in. "Chill, bitch, you know that was an honest fuck-up." He then dialed it back several clicks to a normal conversational tone. "Just hold up for one minute. If we put our minds to it, I bet you we can still salvage this shit."

Herb nodded and grumbled, "Sorry, man. It's all just so frustrating. Maybe if Bud were here, we could pull it off."

"I'll call him. He might have some good news for us." Frank quick-dialed and then waited a few seconds. "Yo, man, what's the news?"

Frank's face gave an answer even before he hung up, but he said it out loud in case it had been overlooked. "No luck finding the parts. He'll be at the airport in the morning."

"That only leaves us twenty-four hours," Herb whined like a bitchy-fuck. "Even if I had those damn drives, that's not near enough time. Fuck it. I give up. I'll just cancel the event."

"We come too far to quit now." Frank shook him by the shoulders. "If we flake, you'll never get those folks to answer your call again."

Herb pulled free and whimpered, "Yeah, they'll be beating down my door after I get them out here for absolutely nothing." He looked down at his toes and mumbled, "I'll be a punch line, man."

"Let's consult the BongRite." Frank smiled and pulled the trigger to direct a steady stream of soothing sativa lungs-ward.

Herb was no longer in arguing mode, so he drowned his sorrows in smoke for several minutes. Then he walked to the landline phone and began punching buttons. "I guess I'll start making some calls. You do an e-mail blast, okay?"

Frank ran over and hung up the phone. "Wait, I just got an awesome idea. We can throw batteries back in and shorten the route."

Herb yanked the phone away. "That won't work. It won't stand up to inspection."

"We'll seal the Love Bus up tight." Frank grinned. "Then we'll tell any interested investors, for further info, they must sign a non-disclosure-agreement. And we'll buy even more time making them notarize it before we can reveal the revolutionary power plant."

"I don't know..." Herb turned to speak toward the Love Bus. "So much could go wrong."

"It's just a stall, bro." Frank smiled and waved an arm in the vehicle's direction. "By the time they jump through all those hoops, we'll have that fucker running perfect."

The alarm buzzer sounded, causing them to reflexively jump-spin and check the security monitors, but they relaxed the instant they saw the box-wielding FedEx messenger fidgeting by the front door.

"That's the tri-fold Love Bus fact sheets for the barbecue."
Herb started for the lobby. "I'll be right back."

When he returned, Herb dropped the package on the ground near the rollup door, then turned and gave a crooked grin. "You know, if we sell it right, that battery stall trick just might work."

Frank nodded, smiled, and pumped his fist. "Let's do it then! But first, let's grab some brews and order take-out. It's gonna be a long night, man."

"Dude, there's twenty cases of Heineken in the rental van."

"Oh yeah," Frank said. "You call in the grub, and I'll go grab a sixer." Right before the doorway, he nudged the FedEx package with his toe. "Should I put these in the van with the party supplies?"

Herb nodded, but in an instant changed his mind. "Wait, I need to check for typos. Crack that box open and hand me one."

Frank whipped out his pocket knife, flicked it open, and sliced through the tape. He peered into the box, and looked more disappointed than a preteen whose parents were getting divorced and blaming it all on him. "Your printers fucked up royally, dude."

Herb groaned, "What's wrong now?"

"They got this shit completely wrong. All that's in here are a couple of ancient computer drives." Frank broke into a grin and held up a floppy drive as he read aloud the accompanying note. "'Sorry, Cuz, couldn't wait around, catfish was jumpin', so I overnighted these. Tried to call, will collect when I see you.'"

Herb rushed over, snatched the box away, and took it to his workbench. "Before we get too excited, I better make sure these are operable."

Frank peered over his shoulder and made stupid little wisecracks as Herb ran a series of tests.

Ten minutes later, Herb unhooked the cables but then just sat in silence.

Three-point-five seconds later, Frank nudged him. "Well?"

"They're in perfect shape," Herb said. "Better than the ones Bud lost."

"So the show goes on?"

Herb nodded. "We might just have enough time. Theoretically, once I install these drives and load software, the Love Bus will be good to go."

"Well then, what the fuck are we waiting for?" Frank smiled while reaching out to high five. "Let's get busy, brother!"

# 18

The next morning, right round sunup, Frank set out to grab Bud from the airport while Herb remained at the workshop, toiling away on Love Bus system controls.

The final systems' analyses were completed with a mere two hours to spare before the event's scheduled start, leaving just enough time for Frank and Bud to run through a pre-unveiling checklist.

Thirty minutes before the invitees' scheduled arrival, Herb took the Love Bus for a quick road test. Even though he expected the worst, it performed like a dream.

With ten minutes to spare, Bud topped off the Love Bus' pot pellet supply, parked the vehicle in the side lot, and then covered her up with a hemp tarp emblazoned with the event's logo: "P.A.R.E. Aiding the Planet."

It was all systems go for the scheduled unveiling ceremony, to be followed by an alternatively-fueled-vehicle parade. Destination, a new paradigm, as well as a lavish barbecue for the press, a few state and local elected officials, venture-capitalists, automotive executives, plus a slew of friends in need.

Out front of the warehouse, lined up facing south along the street, thirty alternatively fueled vehicles stuffed full of passengers – maybe fifty people – sat waiting for the signal to follow the Love Bus' historic drive. Behind the lineup of future-fueled vehicles, nine support vehicles loaded with spare parts, extra batteries, solar panels, and the technicians necessary to keep a green-powered parade moving forward.

In the lot just outside Herb's workshop, twenty-five VIPs and as many friends rubbed elbows as they milled about. The kinetic energy and chattering created an air of excitement much like the first day of school for a nerd, or the final Friday before summer vacation for everyone else.

Just two short days earlier, it seemed as though the moment could never happen. But precisely at the scheduled start time, Herb stood next to the dune buggy, ready to summon the crowds' attention via speakers mounted on the buggy's roll bar.

He raised microphone to mouth and spoke with enough gusto to seize the murmuring crowd's attention. "Alternative-fueled vehicle enthusiasts, may I have your attention please?"

The guests hushed and, except for a few dudes standing behind a honey with an outstanding pooper, all eyes turned toward Herb. Being the center of attention had him smiling like a roofied monkey waking up with a tasty banana up the butt. He waved an arm toward the shrouded Love Bus and sang out in hallelujah fashion, "My friends! Are you ready to change the world? Let me hear you say, 'Yeah!'"

The crowd joined as one exuberant voice with their shouted "Yeah!"

Herb stood taller. His shoulders grew wider as he spoke with more force. "Hell yeah, and thank you one and all." He took a deep bow.

"My name is Herb Gardener, and you all know why I have called you here today. You shall have the honor of being the first to witness the most advanced vehicle this planet has ever known. A vehicle that travels up to twelve hundred miles on sixty dollars' worth of near-zero-emission, domestically produced biofuel, once again proving that progress is the only alternative!"

The crowd clapped and cheered with mounting enthusiasm as Herb whipped the hemp tarp away, revealing the stunning vehicle to satisfy curious eyeballs. All the while, he bellowed like a carnival barker getting plowed by a randy ringmaster. "Behold – the Love Bus, a vehicle that loves the earth as much as Mother Earth loves her!"

The sweet-looking ride got the crowd "oohing" and "aahing" as Herb raised the gull-wing doors via key-fob remote.

Spectators' electric murmuring continued crackling through the lot as he climbed behind the wheel, lowered the doors, and began a pre-operational checklist.

Frank hopped up onto the buggy. He stood tall and proud, smiling with the confidence of a senior quarterback in a room full of drunken freshman cheerleaders as he brought microphone to mouth, surveyed the crowd, sucked up a deep breath, and then roared over the PA like a politician at a whistle stop. "My fellow Americans, right before your very eyes is the future, your future, America's future, the world's future. Today is the day we free ourselves from the shackles of foreign oil while patriotically ridding the scourge of foreign automobiles from our lands. This exceptional nation must refuse to exist beholden to outside control for even one single day forward. With your help and support, we shall once again manufacture world-class, cutting-edge vehicles right here in the good ol' USA, the undisputed car capital of the world!"

Bud erupted, clapping, stomping, wolf-whistling, and cheering, but stopped the instant he noticed everyone silently staring his way.

Frank grinned and shrugged and carried on. "As I was saying, domestically cultivated fuel shall efficiently power these twenty-first century, mass-produced green vehicles. This here Love Bus' breakthrough design – with its beyond-cutting-edge propulsion technology perfected by Mr. Herb Gardener – is destined to bring liberating, high-paying American manufacturing jobs back home."

Frank looked to Herb, who gave the thumbs-up. They both smiled and nodded.

"Good news, folks," Frank roared. "It looks like we're ready to go." He saluted the crowd before winding up his spiel in hyperbole overdrive mode. "From this day forward, April the twenty-second shall be known as Earth *and* Energy Independence Day!"

Everyone began cheering and applauding.

Ka-BOOOOM, Bud blasted a cannon shot over the crowd.

In the blink of a shattered ear drum, frenzied guests hit the ground or scattered, seeking cover.

One by one, and then more and more, folks realized that the deafening blast, with its following massive concussion wave, merely signaled the event's start. So they picked themselves up, brushed off dirt, or any other of a number of ways one gathers wits, and began boarding the limo-bus hired to ferry them to the barbecue.

While Frank and Bud made sure the boarding process moved along smooth and steady, Herb navigated the Love Bus to the front of the parade vehicles lined up along the street.

Fifteen minutes later, with Frank at his side, Bud maneuvered the dune buggy in front of Herb, signaling that all VIPs were on the courtesy coach.

Go time.

Bud gave a "follow me" arm wave then pulled away.

Herb shifted the Love Bus into drive mode and zoomed forward to get within feet of the buggy's bumper.

One by one, the alt vehicles joined in on the parade, pacing the Love Bus, pacing Bud's buggy.

At the corner, they turned right and headed west. Even though Herb claimed the Love Bus as ultra-low-emission, it took Bud several hours to fully mask the exhaust. Despite that effort, every few seconds the slightest wisp of smoke floated out from the back toward the vehicles stretched out behind them for a quarter mile.

Five minutes later, Bud turned right onto the main boulevard and traveled north. From there, it was a fifteen-mile straight shot to the barbecue.

With everything going according to plan, Herb's face had held its smile for the longest period in recorded history. It was a good day.

At about six miles into the history books, two vehicles dropped out of line to park in front of a convenience store. A support vehicle quickly veered off course and got busy getting them back in the game.

Approaching the seven-mile mark, another participant dropped out. The pot-powered parade floated on, and two more technicians would be late to the party.

Right about the ten-mile mark, the Love Bus was letting out more than an occasional faint wisp of exhaust.

Just past the eleven-mile mark, the Love Bus spewed exhaust thicker than a third-world industrial smokestack and began losing speed.

Low visibility amongst the lingering haze caused vehicles to bunch up like an accordion.

It took almost half mile of adjusting speeds to reestablish their spacing. By then the air had begun clearing up, because there was no more exhaust coming from the Love Bus as it rolled to a stop at the curb.

When Bud noticed Herb's troubles in the mirror, he flipped a U-turn, then another, and parked his buggy a few yards in front of the inoperable Love Bus.

Being veteran alternative-fuel aficionados, the rest of the parade seemed to understand if they stopped every time a vehicle quit, they would never get to party. But that knowledge did not prevent most of them from gawking as they inched past.

Bud sprang out of his buggy and hurried to check on a no-longer-smiling Herb, standing alongside the Love Bus.

"I told you putting in a two-way radio wasn't a sidetrack." Bud chuckled and gave him a friendly shove.

Herb swatted at the hand, stomped his foot, and screeched, "Whatever, fuck that shit. Fucking gauge says it's out of fuel."

"Oh, no problem, I'll jet on back to the shop and grab another twenty pounds of pellets." Bud jogged toward his buggy.

Herb's eyes shot open wide as if a giant was squeezing his skull, and they were bulging out like grapes ready to pop as he yelled, "Wait. How much was in there?"

Bud stopped, turned back, and, with a dopey smile, shrugged. "Same amount, bro, twenty pounds."

It looked as though someone dumped a bucket of red paint over Herb's face as he hollered, "What the fu…"

Bud rolled his eyes toward the column of looky-loos crawling past, and Herb stopped hollering mid-explosion.

Back to smiling in an instant, Herb spoke calmly through barely moving lips, "What the fuck are you talking about, Bud? One cup of pellets burned for twelve hours in my control experiment."

Bud cocked his head a wee bit sideways, scratched his butt, and just stood there digesting the situation in silence. It didn't take long to get his goofy smile back. "Oh, I get it, you must've not seen the counter. That MiniBongRite reloaded a ton of times from the main hopper, which holds twenty pounds of pellets, just like the Love Bus. And I guarantee you she got packed chock-full of pellets right after your test drive this morning."

Herb opened the pellet access door to check the fuel supply.

Bud peeked over his shoulder. "Hey, did you figure in all the fuel it takes to cook those pellets?"

Instead of going into full-on ballistic mode, Herb smiled, closed the fuel door, and then gave a friendly wave to a few of the passing alt-fuel cars. All the while, under his breath, he was giving orders. "Just tow your fucking van back to the shop. I'll ride the coach with the VIP folks."

Bud nodded and Herb smiled as he waved at another passing green vehicle

"Do me a favor," Herb pleaded. "When you get to the party, play it off like it was a twenty-dollar part that broke on the prototype. Maybe we can get some of these big wigs drunk and hopefully sell them your piece of shit weed-wasting Bus."

Bud shook his head. "You're on your own in the lying department, bro."

The anger in Herb's eyes boiled like someone who had every promise broken throughout their entire life, yet he put on a warm smile and grumbled, "Fuck you, fucking idiot."

Herb pivoted on his heels one hundred eighty degrees, marched forward, and flagged down the VIP coach.

A minute later, he climbed aboard the coach with that happy, bullshit-smile still plastered across his mug. The door closed and the big bus lurched forward with a hiss.

# 19

Bud mumbled obscenities while hooking a tow rope from his buggy to the disabled Love Bus. After cinching the rope tight, Bud gave it a swift kick. Then he cussed even more while connecting an electrical feed needed to power its steering and brakes.

With Frank behind the wheel of the Love Bus, Bud towed and mumble-cussed the entire trip back to the warehouse.

While the two unhooked the Love Bus in the side parking lot, a familiar voice yelled from behind, "Fuck the planet!"

They turned to see Duke approaching, smiling like a fifty-year-old Fillmore West light show daisy. Alongside him strode another happy, hairy hippie dude.

Bud shouted out with glee, "Duke, you made it! Good to see you, man."

"Sorry we're late, but I couldn't find this place." Duke motioned to his companion. "This is my old friend Omar. He'd dig a pound of that hydro-stuff."

"That can be arranged." Bud smiled and shook hands. "Nice to meet you, Omar."

"Nice for meeting you," said Omar.

Frank got in on the flesh-pressing ritual. "Yo, Duke, we're just here to drop off the Love Bus. Let's do this quick and go party."

"Right on," Duke said while leaning in to take a peek inside the Love Bus. "This is a lovely van. What happened to your big road show?"

Frank shrugged and cryptically explained, "It looked good on paper. But due to some real kooky number-crunching and lack of communication, the demonstration didn't quite go as promised."

Duke looked sadder than a Korean boy whose fat puppy ran away. "That's a shame."

"It's all good." Bud put an arm around the hippie's shoulder. "I'm not really in much of a hurry. Probably better if we kick it here for a while, it'll give my friend Herb time to calm down."

Frank nodded and chuckled. "Then we got all week. Let's head inside and have a smoke – or ten."

Bud laughed and started for the door. "Omar, you got a few different options for that L-B, bro."

Omar stopped his scrutiny of the Love Bus and hurried to catch up. "It sounding most excellent, my friend."

After ending up on the couches in the kickback room, Omar only needed two sample hits to settle on a pound of the delightful "Jack Herer."

With business complete, the time came for Bud to show off his BongRite. "It's simple, just push this button."

A stream of smoke pulled Duke to the edge of his seat trying to catch every last wisp. "That's far out, man."

Bud handed it over so Duke could test-fire the BongRite on his own range. As he smoked his brains out crispier than a brisket in a central Texas BBQ joint, he noticed Frank staring at Omar and released the trigger.

"I'm sorry, I almost forgot." Duke gestured toward his guest. "I didn't tell you kids, but Omar here is a manager of Emir, Ali Bin Oyl Ghowgen's sovereign wealth fund. Ever since I told him about your Love Bus, he's been dying to see it. And possibly make a bid."

Frank smirked while rolling his eyes. "The Emir, huh, that's why you dress so elegantly?"

Omar sat up straight, adjusted the collar of his gravy-stained tie-dyed t-shirt, and spoke forcibly, "Must assure you, my friend, am at Emir's service, with authority comblete for managing affairs of business."

"Sure you are," Frank laughed. "Just hit that button, Ali Baba. I assure you, all will be well."

"My name Omar," he grumbled. "For courtesy to hosts, shall this device brief testing."

While the others got their jones on, Omar sat motionless, expressionless, until Bud hurried him along to green-land with the squeeze of a THC trigger.

A brand-new state of mind blasted his direction, and Omar smiled wider than the east-west cultural gap. "Ah, this magic hookah beautiful more than loveliest three-humbed camel."

"Wow, three humps," Frank laughed. "Talk about stamina."

"Third humbed smog control." Omar broke into a fit of rumbling laughter while slapping Frank on the back. "Ah Ha Ha Ha Ha Ha Ha!"

Frank pushed the slap hand away. "That's actually kind of funny, but quit touching me, bro."

"You kids never really told me," Duke said. "What happened with your Love Bus?"

Bud stared at the ground for a moment before mumbling, "Turns out it costs twenty grand to travel ten miles in a weed-powered 1972 Volkswagen Bus."

Again, Omar erupted into belly jiggling laughter, "Ah Ha Ha Ha Ha Ha Ha!"

Bud blasted away at him until long after the laughter stopped.

Omar wiped his laugh-tears away and said, "When Duke tell me of you bus full of love, am very exciting. Think if were be successful, no longer would infidel army crusaders come drobbing bombs upon my beoples for oil."

"You're looking at it all wrong, man." Frank gave him an oversized Cheshire smile. "Bombing blows shit up, but then they must hire people to rebuild all that blown-up-shit. So bombing creates jobs. If you think about it, American bombers are kind enough to drop jobs from your skies."

"This most untrue, my friend." Omar's friendly expression remained unchanged while his words were emphasized with arms moving about like a traffic cop on Quaaludes. "If you country no addict to betrol, you no would sending crusader missiles at Arab lands."

Frank nodded and took a blast. "That is 100 percent correct, my nomadic friend. You have all the gasoline, but we got the matches. I should point out that foolish OPEC oil embargo started all the geopolitical bullshit. We can't just sit around and let some cartel punk us, right?"

"Guys, guys, chill. Fuck all this politics shit." Bud bounced to his feet. "Let's cut out of here."

Frank offered a dismissive wave of the hand. "There's still plenty of time, dude."

Bud stood hovering, staring, until Frank gave a slight nod indicating he understood it was about time to move along.

Nevertheless, Omar continued explaining the world as seen through his eyes. "You country must seeking first you home oil, so for all to living with beace. Instead, you travel globe for manibulate and bolluting sovereign nations."

Frank shrugged as smoke lazily exited his lungs. "It's an inconvenient truth, buddy. In my country, the environmental whackos have far too much political power, which makes drilling for the vast pools of oil available right here at home not an option. Strangely, these very same people also hate our military. Go figure. I wish they'd just make up their damn minds."

Omar paid very close attention – to the BongRite.

Frank stood and motioned to the door. "We must now leave for the party, buddy."

Omar did not budge, opting instead to enjoy another blast. "Am most comfortable here with magic hookah." Smoke flowed nonstop while the couch attempted to devour him.

"Thank you for the compliment on my BongRiteEndlessHigh," Bud said. "But we must go now. We're hosting a party somewhere else, bro."

"Am understanding, you must elsewhere be host courteous." Omar sat up straight. "But before debart – on behalf Emir, Ali Bin Oyl Ghowgen – wish make offer for burchase, how you say, end bong high smoke, for keebing Emir's harem forever soothed and blump."

Bud chuckled. "Sure, my foreign friend. Ten million bucks and she's all yours. But, 'now it's time to say goodbye to all our company.'"

"Would bayment for gold be accebting, my friend?" Omar stuck a hand out.

Bud grabbed ahold, attempting to pull the overstayer to his feet.

"Ah Ha Ha Ha Ha Ha Ha!" Omar yanked the hand away. "We shake. It deal!"

"You're a funny dude." Bud chuckled and gave a quick toe-to-toe tap to the seated straggler. "But we need to split now."

"You don't have to go home, but you can't stay here." Frank tilted his head skyward and waved an arm toward the heavens. "Go grab your magic carpet and follow us to the party. Then you can give me more details about that harem, buddy."

Omar struggled to his feet. Smiling ear to ear, he bellowed, "You no did say, 'Simon says!'" followed up with a hearty, "Ah Ha Ha Ha Ha Ha Ha Ha!" while jovially slapping Frank's back.

A buzzing alarm drew everyone's attention to the security monitors and the image of A.S.S. agents Thursday and Jefferson prowling about near the Love Bus.

Bud turned to his guests and barked orders like a drill sergeant on downers. "Frank and me gotta deal with this situation out back. You two clear out through the front."

"Who's are they?" asked Duke.

"No time to explain." Bud pointed at the door. "We'll catch up with you at the barbecue."

Frank retrieved his trusty baseball bat from under the couch and thumped the lumber in his palm. "What's the plan, buddy-boy?"

With index finger pointed skyward, Bud swept his arm in a circular motion. "Show these guys out then come around from the front and seal off any escape. I'll watch on my iPad and cut them A.S.S. fuckers off when I see you closing in."

Frank ceased the hopping in place, bat waggling to pause for the focusing calm of a long, deep breath. Then, with a wave of an arm, he started for the door. "Okay – Duke, Omar, get the fuck out."

Duke had no issue doing as instructed, but Omar held his ground to bend at the waist while twirling his forearm forward into an outstretched palm. "My friend, am…"

Frank grabbed the arm, trying to drag him out.

Omar jerked and tugged to break free, while demanding, "At once must let go. Am wishing you assist with broblem men."

"That's what you're doing, bro." Frank set him loose and held the door. "I'll tell you what you can do right after we get out front."

Omar nodded before scurrying past Frank, who turned back inside and flashed thumbs-up.

Bud returned the thumbed gesture and bolted for the workshop.

# 20

Twenty-one seconds later, Bud stood just inside the backdoor with eyes glued to tablet screen, tracking Thursday and Jefferson slowly circling the Love Bus. "C'mon, Frank. Where the fuck are you?"

Another forever passed by in sixty seconds, but when Thursday approached the buggy to give the steering wheel a quick yank-twist, Bud burst out the back door, yelling, "You two, hold it right there!"

A quarter of an instant after Bud sprang from the doorway, Thursday and Jefferson took off quicker than a blur riding a cheetah. Bud gave chase for several hundred yards, until the A.S.S. men made it to their car and sped off.

A few seconds later, Bud hyper-vent-a-yelled into the phone, "Where... the fuck... are you, dude? They got away."

Bud listened briefly, kicked at the ground, and pleaded, "Well, just get... back... there, now, okay?"

When Bud arrived back to the warehouse, Frank was halfway down the block, jogging toward him. So Bud took an opportunity to flip him off before stepping into the lot.

The moment Frank stepped through the gate, Bud yelled, "What the fuck? We had them boxed in."

Frank's hand flapped with the talk, talk, talk gesture. "Sorry, man, got sidetracked with that Omar dude."

"Yeah, I'm sure you had nothing to add." Bud slammed his foot into the Love Bus' rear tire. He then winced, followed by a deep breath and heaving sigh. "What a shitty fuckin' day, bro."

"Dude, calm down," Frank said. "We know right where they're going."

"I was looking forward to home field advantage," Bud said.

Frank waggled his bat. "I'm undefeated on the road."

Bud un-slouched and his frown turned upside down. "Alrighty then!" He gave an energetic fist pump and sprinted for the dune buggy, hollering, "To the Buggy-Mobile, Robin!"

Frank made a mad dash for the driver's seat. "I want to be, Batman, fucker."

He wasn't quite quick enough, because Bud hopped behind the wheel and laid down the law. "I'm driving, so you're Robin, bitch."

Frank stomped a foot and whined like a petulant preteen who downed seven energy drinks. "Robin drove sometimes."

"Like ten yards, once!" Bud yelled over the rumbling exhaust. "If it'll make you feel better, you can be Alfred."

A few seconds of pouting later, Frank threw up his arms and gave in. "Well, okay, I guess it's better than being your little bat-twink."

"Sometimes!" Bud hollered. "But don't knock it till you try it, bro."

"I don't know," said Frank. "I watched some gay porn once." He rubbed his ass. "It didn't look that fun."

Bud gave a roll of the eyes and handed over the tablet. "Just get the gate, bro. Once I pull out, close up and tap the padlock icon. That'll seal this place up tighter than a vault."

"Okay, let's hit the road." Frank ran to pull the gate wide open, and as the buggy puttered by he yelled, "Hey what's this icon, 'Corn Recipes'?"

Bud's face dropped quicker than a lead balloon off a cliff as he screamed, "Don't touch that!"

Unfortunately, Frank had tapped the icon while asking the question. His action's reaction, loud booming pops accompanied by the hissing sounds of deflating tires, made him look for a place to hide away. "Oh, it's for spike strips; forgot about those," he mumbled.

Bud slammed on the brakes and wailed, "Fuuuuuck, man, shi-i-i-i-t!" then leaned his forehead against the steering wheel for a moment before looking back to the gate. "You can tap that again any time now."

Frank double tapped the corn cob icon, triggering the row of sharp metal claws protruding from the ground to snap back into ready position.

Bud jerked the shifter into reverse and plop-plop-plopped the buggy back inside the lot. He jumped out and stomped to the rear of the vehicle to snatch the tablet away.

"Not fair," Frank said. "You know I love corn."

Bud pounded his fist on the fender. "Aaugh!"

"Corn recipes, seriously? Who does that?" Frank got busy rib tickling his dejected buddy.

Bud never could resist the tickle monster, so he giggled and pulled away. "Fuck it. Guess it's just one of those days, bro."

"I'm totally sorry, man," Frank said. "I won't pull the football away again, promise. What's the new, new plan?"

"Help me put the stock rims back on her." Bud said. "I think way better while working."

"We can always cruise there in the Love Bus," Frank suggested.

"Good idea," Bud said. "It's close enough to round-trip."

Frank started for the workshop. "I'll go grab a sack of pellets."

Twenty minutes later, the Love Bus was refueled and the guys were cruising along in a sweet-looking vehicle that pumped out more smoke than a Chinese steel mill.

Frank asked, "How you want to do this shit, man?"

"I was thinking." Bud gestured over his shoulder. "We'll hook a hose to that pellet-burner and feed it through their mail slot. Those fuckers might be a bit more pliable if we smoke them out first."

"Oh, *that's* what the hose is for." Frank snapped his wrist to crack that whip. "I thought we were going to beat them with it."

"I hope it doesn't come to that." Bud turned to make direct eye contact. "Let's try the friendly approach first, okay?"

Frank grabbed the bat resting between his thighs and winked. "How about you speak softly, and I'll keep them aware of the big stick ready to party."

"That's kinda close to what I was thinking," Bud said. "But I need you to be subtle."

"What's that word you say, 'sub-tell?'" Frank grinned. "Me no speaky."

"Whatever." Bud pleaded, "Just don't start thumping on them unless I give you the high sign."

"Like this?" Frank waved his arms in the long, flailing strokes of a drunken albatross.

Bud smiled and shook his head. "Not quite, but you'll know it when you see it, bro."

Frank pointed ahead about half a block. "Let's grab some donuts, in case we have to stake out that place."

"Good idea." Bud took a quick peek over his shoulder and then cranked a hard left into the strip mall, home to a wonderful establishment providing delectable donuts to a munch-crazed-world.

Mere seconds after they parked, a few teenagers arrived on bicycles and gathered round the Love Bus. One of the boys gave a thumbs-up, while another signaled an A-OK. Bud responded with a smiling nod.

"I'll run in," Frank said. "That little Asian babe in there loves me."

"No time for that." Bud employed the arm bar. "Wait here and keep an eye on the car. I'll be right out."

A few minutes later, Bud set a pink box on the seat before climbing in and swatting Frank's hand away from the treats.

"Dude, I just wanted to see," Frank complained.

"I don't want your grubby hands on them until I get mine," Bud said.

Behind the Love Bus, clustered near the no-longer-secret exhaust port, the freelance ganja groupies had grown to half a dozen.

Bud, preoccupied by donut-guarding duty, nearly backed over them, causing the motley crew to scatter for their bicycles as the Love Bus pulled away. Like a Pied-Pot-Piper, the kids pedaled furiously to keep in contact with high-dollar. stinky-sweet exhaust fumes.

When a red light stopped the Love Bus, those bike brats were on its bumper within seconds. Bud was focused straight ahead while tapping a beat upon the steering wheel, so remained unaware of the gathered crowd. A check of the mirror alerted him to the wee lads, plus three folks from the nearby bus stop, wrestling one another out of the way to get closest to the smoke. "Dude, check out that shit behind us."

Frank took a gander over his shoulder. "Man, oh man, buddy-boy. Just like you in junior high."

Bud wore a double-dopey grin, boasting, "By the time I was their age, I already had me a crop of Chronic ready for market."

The light turned green and he stomped the accelerator. "Let's lose them fuckers."

It was no use. By the next red light, the kids had caught up. "Dammit," Bud whined. "We got shit to do."

"I got an idea." Frank pointed ahead. "Pull into that 7-Eleven."

When the light changed, Bud directed the Love Bus into the convenience store's lot, where Frank told him, "Back up to the front doors and leave her running till I say."

Frank stepped from the vehicle as the bicycle cannabis club reformed to partake in all the smoke near the rear. He gave a nod as he passed by, then propped the store's doors wide open and took a casual stroll to the counter. After a brief conversation with the clerk, he handed over some cash and set off for the back of the establishment.

Not three minutes later, Frank returned with four large bags of chips, placed them on the counter, and walked to the door to wave an arm toward the Love Bus.

When Bud caught his eye in the mirror, Frank slid a finger across his throat. Signal received, Bud killed the power and the spewing smoke stopped, but the fog rolling inside made the store's interior resemble summer in San Francisco.

Frank turned to salute the clerk, who ripped open a Slim Jim, giggled a little and waved the crowd inside.

After hurrying back to his seat, Frank karate-chopped forward. "Let's get the fuck out of here."

Bud mashed pedal to metal, sending the Love Bus lurching forward like an O-lineman at the snap. "How'd you do that?"

Frank began unwrapping a mini peanut butter cup. "Never underestimate the power of free chips and Slurpees for all my friends."

With a quick right out of the lot, Bud sped down a side street and took the first left. After jogging over block by block toward their destination, his tactic served the desired elusive purpose.

About a mile from the 7-Eleven, Bud once again checked mirror for urchins before hanging a right onto the street where the A.S.S. office was located. While they rolled along, Frank's hand spider-walked toward a stealthy attack on the donut box.

Watching from the corner of his eye, Bud readied to swat the pilfering hand away for the seventh time, but instead pointed through the windshield and sounded the alarm. "Holy sheep shit, they're right there!"

A.S.S.'s gate was wide open. Right out front of the office, agents Thursday and Jefferson stood with backs to the street, unaware of the whisper-quiet Love Bus nearby.

Frank aborted the snack attack to grasp his bat with both hands, readying for an all-out A.S.S. assault. "Fuck waiting around all night. Let's just do this."

"Right on, bro." Bud cranked the wheel toward the property's entrance. "Remember, be mellow."

His focus locked on the targets ahead, Frank said, "No promises, buddy-boy."

Five feet from the men, Bud slammed on the brakes for effect. Anti-lock brakes foiled his skid, because the Love Bus came to an ultra-smooth, quiet halt. He activated the gull-wing doors and stepped out. "Hello, fellas. I was wondering if there was anything we could do for you?"

The hum of doors spreading open got the A.S.S. men's attention. Thursday even appeared slightly amused as he spoke. "I'm glad you have finally decided to respond to our summons, son."

Bud stopped in his tracks. "What summons?"

Frank, having paused long enough to scarf down a donut in two bites, licked icing from his fingertips and jumped out to run toward the men while waving the Louisville Slugger. "Why do you cops keep fucking with us?"

"We're not police... we're parking." Jefferson pointed to a sign – Automotive Storage Systems – above the bungalow's door.

Frank halted the advance and gazed upward to take a few moments examining the sign, but could only muster a weak, "Oh, right, then. Parking it is."

Bud glanced at the sign and scratched his noggin as the shifting winds redirected smoke pouring from the Love Bus, engulfing the quartet within a cannabis cloud.

It wasn't too long before the winds of change once again took a new direction. The clearing air motivated Jefferson to approach the smoke's source, where he squatted down and took a few deep breaths. He then stood, smiling as smoke drifted from his mouth to nostrils.

"Guess I better shut her down." Bud stepped toward the Love Bus.

"Hold up there for a minute, son." Thursday scurried to Love Bus to partake in several deep inhales of his own.

With the dopey smile of a proud pothead, Bud joined the A.S.S. men at the Love Bus' rear. "Looks like I invented me a mobile, industrial BongRite."

Bud enjoyed a few tokes before shutting down the Love Bus, causing Thursday and Jefferson to climb over one another in a vain attempt to corral the final whiffs of pot smoke drifting up, up, and away.

"You guys done?" Bud yelled out. "We need to clear things up."

All smiles, Jefferson slouched down to rest an arm on his partner's shoulder. "I disagree. What we really need is to get some Cheetos – ASAP, brother."

Thursday gave him a quick elbow jab to the ribs. "And hot dogs, partner."

Bud rubbed his belly. "I could eat. But not till I get some fuckin' answers."

Frank withdrew a pack of pineapple gummy bears from his pocket and dangled them at the A.S.S. men, who snapped to attention and followed the candy like a hypnotist's watch.

After some begging and pleading, Frank provided each man with a single gummy. He followed up with an offer the stoned could never refuse: "There's more where that came from, plus I got a line on some éclairs and old-fashioned donuts. But only if you spill it."

Thursday wiped a spot of drool from the corner of his mouth. "You had me at 'éclair.' What do you want to know?"

Bud asked, "Do you guys have my Camaro?"

"That depends," said Thursday. "Are you Al Yalikakik?"

Frank lifted the bat and stepped forward. "How'd you like a kick, fucker?"

Jefferson's smile disappeared faster than a wallet in a whorehouse as he sized up Frank, looking for an opening to pounce.

Bud stuck an arm out to block the advance. "Calm down, bro." He caught Frank's eye and gave a wink. "That's the dude I bought her from."

"Oh yeah," said Frank with a chuckling two steps backward.

"If that's the case, I do believe we have your vehicle," Thursday said.

"Well, I want her back," Bud demanded. "Right this fuckin' minute, bro."

"As soon as you pay all the related fees," Thursday said, "the car's all yours."

Bud howled like a little dog in a room full of big bitches in heat. "Fuckin' pay for what?"

"Unpaid parking fees," came Thursday's calmer-than-calm reply.

"That's total bullshit." Bud went for his phone. "If I don't get my fuckin' car back right now, I'm calling 911."

Jefferson looked to his partner and gave a slight nod before chiming in. "We have surveillance video of the incident in question."

Frank raised the bat halfway. "Sure you do."

"No need for that, son." Thursday waved an arm and turned toward the building's entrance. "If you two care to come inside, I will show you the video."

Bud signaled Frank to whoa it up and followed Thursday inside.

Frank wasn't too far behind, and once he stepped through the doorway, Thursday motioned for the guys to take a seat. "Give me a minute to pull up the pertinent footage."

Standing in the doorway, Jefferson called out to his partner, "I'll be right outside if you need me."

Frank looked to Bud, put finger to eye, and tracked the departing Jefferson. "Be right back. I'll grab those donuts."

Jefferson slammed on the brakes and spun, facing Frank. "If you try anything, I'll shove that bat up your fucking ass."

The bat-wielding arm fell to his side. Frank looked him eye to chin while holding up his free hand. "We're cool, buddy. Just going to put this in the van and grab some munchies."

Jefferson paused for a serious moment before proceeding outside. Frank then waited for a couple more skipped heartbeats before making his own exit.

While Bud twiddled his thumbs, Thursday focused on the computer screen. It didn't take very long for Thursday to find what he was searching for. "Here we go. What we have here is video from the exit gate, Lot G at Bob Hope Airport."

Bud scooted closer and leaned in. On screen, captured in glorious high definition, Herb was kneeling down by an automated payment machine. After a few seconds of tinkering with keypad and credit card slot, the exit gate swung up and Herb scurried out of camera view.

Seconds later, a classic Camaro with a clear shot of the front license plate – plus a grinning-ear-to-ear Herb behind the wheel – sped toward the exit.

Thursday froze the video. "It's apparent that is not you operating the vehicle. So I will need to see documentation – proof of ownership – before I can release the hold."

Bud stood and nodded. "Not a problem, I got all that shit back at the pad."

"Glad we were able to clear up this matter." Thursday reached out to shake hands.

"Right on, I guess we owe you a few bucks." Bud offered back a hand in peace. "What's the damage, man?"

"Just a minute, I'll get those numbers for you." Thursday clicked open a spreadsheet file. After a few mouse wheel scrolls, plus some sporadic keyboard tapping, he reported, "Well, the airport parking fees are twenty-eight dollars."

Bud let out a ginormous sigh of relief and dug into a front pocket to retrieve his Betty Boop money clip.

"Hold on there, son," said Thursday. "Before you get too excited, there's still the matter of impound fees and fines."

"So how much is that gonna be?" Bud grumbled.

A quick check of the bottom line later, Thursday delivered some harsh news. "Which, as of today, you're looking at four thousand, nine hundred, nineteen dollars and sixty cents."

Bud tensed up like a brick was moving ever so slowly past his sphincter, causing him to try the whimpering approach. "You can't just hold my car hostage like that. This is the first time I heard of this shit."

"That's not my concern," Thursday said. "We've been mailing 'friendly reminder' notices every six weeks."

Bud's clenched fist hammered the desktop. "Dammit, I never received nothing!" he screeched. "That's totally fucked, bro."

"Calm down, son," Thursday urged. "As a courtesy, within a week of the airport scam, my partner and I paid a visit to the vehicle's registration address to collect the fees. But from the intercom were told," he checked his notes, "Quote, 'Fuck off, I don't owe you parking Nazis shit!' Subsequently, my partner and I were threatened with physical harm to several generations of our families."

"Fuckin' Herb," grumbled Bud.

Thursday referred to his notes once more before continuing. "You arrived in target vehicle not more than twenty seconds later." His eyes darted to and fro, scanning the screen. "Here it is, a 1969 RS/SS convertible Camaro, California license plate FAUXCUE, correct?"

Bud nodded. "That's her."

"I can assure you, young man, upon the vehicle's arrival, we attempted to gain your attention," Thursday said. "But you were already inside the building by the time we made it to the door."

"It's total bullshit. You guys can't just take my car like that."

"We have every legal right to acquire collateral," Thursday said. "People really should read the parking stub. It's a contract."

"Gee, thanks for the tip." Bud sprang to his feet. "I still think you guys could have made more effort," he whined. "Five grand is ridiculous."

Thursday's expression turned dour, straight into almost menacing as he raised his voice. "We tried to clear things up several months ago. But once you guys decided to electrocute me, it was 'no more Mr. Nice guy.'"

Bud's huge grin was met by a massive scowl. So he dropped the smirk and went with a sympathetic tone, "Oh yeah, sorry bout that shit, bro."

Thursday stood, and actually managed a smile. "Apology accepted. Are there any more questions, son?"

"Nah, fuck it," Bud said. "Guess I'm screwed. I'll bring you that cash, and some proof of ownership, tomorrow. But only after I see that my baby's okay."

"Not a problem." Thursday made his way to the door. "It's right out in the lot."

With a bounce in his step, Bud was right on Thursday's heels. Just past the doorway, Thursday shaded his eyes while checking left to right and calling out, "Jefferson, where'd you go, partner?"

Bud gave him a nudge and set off for the Love Bus, where he tapped on the glass. As the doors rose up, an arena-sized smoke cloud escaped skyward. There at the wheel sat Frank savoring a donut. Alongside him, Jefferson attempting to cram a smoking rubber hose into his left nostril.

"Wipe that shit off," Bud commanded. "Then pass it, bro."

Thursday gave him a pat on the back. "I'll go grab a couple chairs, son."

Four former adversaries spent the next half hour passing the peace pipe, and forgiving while forgetting. When Bud checked the time on his phone, he jumped to his feet and cried out. "Fuck, we gotta get to the barbecue before all the ribs are gone."

# 21

A good-time party was still raging on when Frank and Bud arrived to the barbecue. With free weed, booze, and smoked meats, it was no big surprise that not a single guest uttered even a sideways word about the Love Bus' performance issues. Nevertheless, buzzkill Herb was in full-tilt bitch mode.

So after a few beers, some smoked brisket, and several barbecued baby-back ribs, Frank and Bud left Herb to his lonesome, to later bellyache about having to wrap up everything all on his own.

Mid-morning, two days after the Love Bus parade's abrupt ending, Bud had just finished tending to the crops. Meaning it was BongRite hour.

When Bud stepped into the kickback room, he spotted Herb camped out on the couch with the BongRite nozzle on full throttle, and quite possibly Velcroed to his face.

With head held low, Bud continued moving toward the workshop. But life's never that easy. Herb called out, "I saw the counter on my workbench, and your fucking contraption reloaded pellets more than three hundred times during my tests."

Bud turned around. Avoiding eye contact, he semi-shrugged and offered an apology in the form of, "Oops," while shuffling backward a few inches closer to solitude.

"That's all you got?" Herb yelled. "Fuck, 'Oops!' You fucked me up big time."

"How many times I gotta say sorry till you get over it?" Bud placed his palms together in prayer alignment and took a backward step.

Herb ripped the BongRite away and leaned forward to lay his forehead atop his knees and whimper, "There's nothing you can say, man."

Almost to the shop's door, Bud looked at crybaby Herb, took a glance over his shoulder to the door of freedom, then back to his friend breaking down on the sofa. Bud let out an annoyed sigh, followed by the encouraging words, "We'll get through this rough patch. You'll see, bro."

Herb twisted his head, resting an ear on his knee. "'Rough patch' is an understatement. Don't you think?"

"It's not all doom and gloom," Bud said. "I got some good news – got my badass Chevy back."

Herb sat up, threw his arms in the air and hollered, "How does that fix a thing, dude?"

"Well, those A.S.S. guys had it." Bud took a few steps toward the couches. "And the good news is they're not cops."

"Well that's good news for you, I guess." Herb took a blast.

"Hate to break it to you." Bud crept a few feet closer to the allure of couch and BongRite. "But you owe me for the impound fees, bro."

"I'm not paying your fucking impound fees," Herb scoffed. "It's not my fault your car got towed."

Eyes locked in on the smoke-pumping nozzle, Bud leaned in like a cartoon bear getting a whiff of picnic basket. "Actually, it's all your fault, bro."

"How do you figure?" Herb asked.

Bud abandoned his escape plan and plopped down onto the sofa to wrestle the BongRite away. "You remember borrowing my car last fall, to go to the airport?"

"Yeah, so?" Herb asked. "What's that got to do with the price of tea in China?"

Bud cackled a bit before explaining the details, in a way that even a smart person might understand. "Well, you see, when you returned from your Las Vegas lose-quest, penniless, they caught you on video driving off – in my car, fucker – without paying two day's worth of parking fees."

No rebuttal was offered. Herb merely stopped fidgeting about and tugged on the BongRite's hose. "Let go, dude."

Unwilling to give up the smoke, Bud moved the nozzle to the other hand. "Have you been throwing out letters from Automotive Storage Systems?"

Herb's sheepish grin came with a nod.

"That's what I thought," said Bud. "Unfortunately, they took my car as ransom, so you owe me about five grand, bro."

Herb punched at the air, causing a swirl in the cloud hovering above. "No way, that's ridiculous!" he roared.

"I got a receipt for you." Bud handed off the BongRite. "You're just lucky Frank and me got them guys wasted, because for a pound of pellets they knocked twelve hundred off the total. Plus half a pack of gummy bears; you owe Frank a buck fifty."

"You got a lot of nerve," Herb whined. "Because of you I'm flat broke. I'll probably be forced to sell my warehouse."

"Take some responsibility," Bud said. "You gotta pay me back, bro."

"I just don't have it. Truth is, I'll probably be homeless soon." Herb leaned forward once again, making no attempt to hide his sobs.

"You're being overdramatic." Bud made a sweeping gesture toward the wall dividing kickback room from grow space. "We got a massive crop ready next week. That'll give us some cash flow."

Herb sat up, wiped his eyes with a shirt sleeve, and whimpered, "Still going to be ultra-tight, man."

"Dude, you got tons of high-dollar shit lying around here," Bud said. "Just liquidate some of it."

While Bud blasted him, Herb looked around the room from one semi-valuable item to another. After a minute of smoke-soaked pondering, he said, "The only thing worth anything is your piece of shit weed-wasting bus. I guess I could put the batteries back in and sell it."

"Probably get fifty grand for her, easy." Bud smiled and made the money sign with thumb and forefinger. "Then you can pay me back."

"That's less than half of what I sunk into that motherfucker!" Herb screeched. "And, between the parade and the hopper in the workshop, you burned up almost forty thousand dollars' worth of pellets, asshole."

"Hey, man, it was your project. I was just helping out a friend." Bud burped some smoke and grinned. "So I'll say it once again – oops."

"You're such a fucking prick." Herb pumped up his volume. "Just put the God damn batteries back in. I'll decide what to do with it then."

Bud sat up enough to facilitate a gentle arm flailing while using his persuasive voice. "Hey, bro, how about instead of using batteries, let's run it off the fuel tank already inside her? The one we used for igniting the pot pellets."

"Not a chance in hell." Herb lowered his voice several notches to plead, "So quit arguing and get the job done."

Bud tried selling his plan with a little more gusto. "But if we leave that tank in there, we got an unlimited supply of free fuel."

"There is no such thing." Herb bolted to his feet and leaned in close enough to say and spray it. "I'm sick of dealing with your idiocy. I'll be at Kat's."

As Herb stormed off toward the workshop, Bud raised his middle finger, but decided rather quickly his hand would be better served operating a self-contained pot smoking device.

Bud kept an eye on the monitor, watching Herb pace the side parking lot. Almost immediately after Herb's girlfriend pulled up to the gate, the two of them drove off.

After scraping himself from the couch, Bud dug out his phone and headed for the workshop. Walking along, using his happy voice, spittle flecks dotted the phone's screen as he reported, "Hey, bro, coast is clear. Get over here and help me stick some batteries in the Love Bus. I want to be done with that shit so I can start working on a pocket-sized BongRite."

Bud paused for a moment before disagreeing. "I don't think it'll be that dangerous."

A few seconds later, he chuckled. "Whatever. I'll see you in a few."

Within the hour, Bud had jettisoned most of the unnecessary small shit from within the Love Bus. Right about the time he began unbolting the fuel tank and pellet burner, there was a knock upon the back door.

Less than fifteen minutes after Frank's arrival, the last of the pot power plant was gone from within the Love Bus.

With the interior cleared out, Bud went to check the battery packs charging on a table. "These are good to go. I'll get inside so you can hand them to me one at a time."

Frank had made other plans, so he waved Bud over to the BongRite. "Break time, buddy."

"Right on." Bud rubbed his chest and smiled like a plumber in a porno. "I could smoke."

In between blasts, Frank ogled the Love Bus from stem to stern and back again, all the while smiling. "I know it all turned into a giant clusterfuck, but the project was actually kind of fun."

Bud looked to the door, checked the monitors, and then took another quick peek at the door. "Don't tell Herb, but I had a blast building that fuckin' ride."

"Is that why you never punched him in the nose?" Frank did a little shadow boxing.

"I'm a lover, not a fighter." Bud put an arm around his shoulder.

"It's possible to be both, buddy-boy," said Frank with a grin and a pat on the back.

"Speaking of punching him in the nose." Bud threw a quick combo jab at the air. "Fuckin' Herb gave me major grief about paying me back for my Camaro."

"At least now we don't have to worry about A.S.S. busting us." Frank reached for the smoke nozzle. "It's still fucked that we don't know what's up with the actual cop."

Bud shuddered. "Fuck, I actually almost forgot about him."

"I say we call to find out what he wants," said Frank.

"Herb don't want me to," Bud grumbled, kicked his leg out, and then made a quick jackknife forward to stop from flipping backward.

"He told – you – not to call, dude," Frank said.

"Don't wanna piss him off anymore." Bud held out his phone. "So, whatever you do, don't call Sergeant Halen."

Frank strode across the way to Herb's workbench, where he got busy rifling through the piles of paper littering it. Near the middle of the third pile, he stopped paper shuffling and bent down to look closer. An exuberant "Aha!" accompanied the waving of a business card high above his head.

While walking back to his chair, Frank punched in the digits. Four seconds later, he offered greetings. "Yes, hello, may I speak to Stan Halen, please?"

Following a wink at Bud, Frank said, "Great, well my name is Herb Gardner. A few months back you left your card at my place of business, requesting I get in touch. I must sincerely apologize for taking so long to return your call. It's been crazy over here."

Almost immediately, Frank's face melted into the worried look of one who had bet against Oprah. "You say you need to speak to Frank Odious?"

He tried solving his problems by passing off the phone, but Bud pushed the incoming hand away and whispered, "Say something, fucker."

Frank drew a deep breath before returning phone to ear, and then lied like some good pussy was at stake. "I have no idea when I will see Mr. Odious again. I believe he moved out of state. If he calls, I can surely pass along a message for you."

Moments later, Frank's face relaxed straight into a slight smile. "Well, to be completely honest with you, this is Frank speaking."

A few seconds later, Frank was smiling like a surfer receiving news of a gnarly swell coming. "Sorry about lying to you, sir," he said. "I promise it won't happen again."

About two more seconds of listening led him to shoot a frown in Bud's direction. "As a matter of fact," Frank said, "he's right here beside me."

Bud's arms waved about like a dodo bird tossed from a helicopter.

"Sure, I can give him a message." Frank turned to Bud. "He wants you to stay away from Lilly, bro."

Bud put a thumb up and nodded.

"You have Bud's word," Frank said. "Give him about two hours, and he will never again shag your little girl."

Bud drove a fist into Frank's arm and yanked the phone away. "Hello, Sergeant, sir, this is Bud." After listening while his face worried, Bud begged, "No, no, please, Frank's an idiot. I swear, sir, I never touched your daughter. It's 100 percent innocent. I assure you that I like women, not girls."

It was more than a minute before Bud got an opportunity to speak again. "Right on… I mean yes, sir! And thank you very much for understanding."

Not long after receiving the phone back, Frank's face broke into a giant grin. He started to say something, but didn't quite get it out, so he continued listening.

Along the way, he managed to blurt, "No thanks. I appreciate the offer, but…"

When allowed to speak again, Frank did so in a respectful tone. "Really, I'm flattered, sir. But I'll have to pass. Thanks again, Sergeant."

Frank started to move the phone away from his ear, but stopped abruptly. "Oh yeah. I think, maybe, if you were to look behind the big rock by the front door where you left your card, you might find some Kush that the local street toughs stashed."

After listening for a moment, Frank waved his free hand. "No charge, buddy. Thanks again, and I mean it." He hung up the phone and reached for the BongRite.

Bud watched and waited for three whole seconds before punching Frank's arm. "Well?" Bud asked.

"Sergeant Halen just wanted a half dub of Kush," Frank said. "Something about how freaky it makes his wife. And, 'Oh, the things she'll do.'"

Bud exhaled for only the fifth time in the previous few minutes. "That's a fuckin' relief, bro. What was that 'no thanks' all about?"

"I was politely declining an offer to join him and the wife in some bedroom sport." Frank said. "His ol' lady doesn't look that great half-naked."

Bud thrust his fist upward. "He wanted to play cops in rubbers with you, huh?"

"Yup, to protect and serve," Frank said, and then a grin spread across his face. "I think I'll switch up the Kush for Bubonic. That way I can follow him around to get some photos we can use later."

"C'mon, bro, you're almost better than that," Bud said. "Just be happy he's not trying to bust us."

"Whatever, guess you got a point." Frank stood and made his way to the kickback room's door. "I'll go stash that Kush for Halen to 'find.' Then let's get these fucking batteries done and cruise to the titty bar."

"Right on," said Bud.

After spending most of the afternoon re-electrifying the Love Bus, the guys went for a test cruise and then enjoyed a few happy hours at a fine establishment featuring "Chicas Chicas Chicas."

Almost immediately after the Love Bus returned to the warehouse's side parking lot, Frank hopped out and laughed. "I need to mark this day on my calendar, buddy-boy."

As Bud scurried for the entrance, he turned back to ask, "Why for, bro?"

Frank urged him to keep moving. "I think this is the first time I've ever seen you weed-less."

Bud fumbled with the lock then yanked the door open. "I forgot all about it until we invited them strippers to check out our weed mobile."

With a mad rush for the nearest BongRite, Bud's wobbly hands retrieved the business end to begin blasting all his trembles away.

At the other BongRite station, Frank pulled the trigger and got in on destroying some of his own brain cells. Seconds later, he gazed through the dense smoke, ogling the monitor displaying the Love Bus. "I can't believe we did all that work just to make a battery-powered VW Bus."

Bud took a gander at yonder monitor. "Even though I liked it better as a mobile BongRite, it wasn't all wasted time. She's got a seventy-mile range – with a twenty-four-hour charge."

Frank shrugged. "Well, I guess that's pretty neat for doing nearby errands."

"Plus an electric Love Bus is way faster off the line than a stock VW Bus." Bud paused for a warm, refreshing blast of bliss before adding, "It does pretty much suck that all those batteries take up so much space she won't haul much cargo anymore."

"Yeah, you can fit three whole bags of groceries in there." The buzzing alarm stopped Frank mid-laugh. He pointed at the monitor. "Who the fuck is that?"

"Fuckin' homeless guy wants to Dumpster dive," Bud said. "I forgot to lock the gate."

"I'll go run him off." Frank hurried to the door. "If I'm not back in five minutes, it means that bum has a cute, younger sister."

On the monitor, Bud watched Frank jump back from the trespasser who had attempted to kiss his cheek. "Oh, it's only Omar," Bud said.

In the parking lot, Frank and Omar did the dance of lively conversation as they moved around then disappeared behind the Love Bus. When they reentered the camera's view near the entrance gate, Omar waved an arm in a "come-this-way" gesture. Seconds later, a full-sized van pulled into the lot and parked a few feet from the building.

Bud headed for the door, swung it open, and reached out to shake hands. "Good to see you, Omar. You come back for a re-weed-load?"

Wearing a jolly smile, the unexpected guest leaned in and placed kisses upon Bud's cheeks. "Salutations, my friend," said Omar. "Am still having most Jack Hairer buds, but would no argue if were to sell one more same."

"Not a problem. Any time, bro," Bud said.

"Of most imbortant, am coming for magic hookah," said Omar.

Bud stepped aside and waved Omar in. "Let's get to it then."

The trio settled in at the nearest BongRite, where Bud passed a nozzle to his guest.

"You remember, no?" Omar said. "We have deal. Come for buying of magic hookah."

"Oh yeah," said Bud with a laugh and a pat on the back. "But you're ten million shy of a full deck, dude."

"Am no understanding, you, 'shy full deck.'" Omar shrugged then got busy blasting himself.

Frank nudged Bud, made a silly face, and they both got a bit of a chuckle.

Omar's ears wiggled as he removed finger from trigger. With eyeballs bouncing about like super balls in a clothes dryer, he withdrew a phone from his pocket. Soon he was speaking in a foreign tongue, sounding quite a bit like "Blah-la-la-la-lah."

He hung up without waiting for a reply, stuck a thumb in the air, and got right back to smoking.

"I'll go grab that L-B, bro." Bud started off toward the kickback room.

Upon his return with the pound of premium pot, Bud said, "You know, bro, if you were to buy five units at a time, you'd save yourself a grand."

Omar opened the zip seal, stuck his oversized nose into the bag, and inhaled deeply. "Ahhhhhhh," he cooed. "Most excellent, habibi."

"That strain's one of my favorites," Bud said.

Omar lifted the BongRite nozzle. "For how long lasting the hookah?"

"Not that long," said Bud. "We use pot pellets in the BongRite."

A blank stare prompted Bud to explain, "That's what I call the 'magic hookah.'"

Omar came alive with a wide smile. "Oh, most excellent, my friend. Must ask, what are 'bot bellets'?"

"I'll show you, bro." Bud walked toward the pellet hopper and waved an arm. "Come over here and check this shit out, bro."

After a brief show and tell, Omar stuck his hand into the hopper, dug up a handful of pellet-formed pot, and let them fall through his fingers. "How much costing, for the bellets?'"

Bud laughed. "Depends on how much you want."

Omar looked to Bud as if he were staring at a glue-sniffing two-year-old with Down syndrome. "Of course, shall require all the bellets."

A thunderous boom of a door knock compelled Bud to jump-spin toward the monitor. The discovery of two titans in dark suits and darker glasses right outside the back door had Bud preparing himself for flight out the front.

Omar put a hand on Bud's shoulder, preventing launch. "No worry, okay," Omar reassured him before turning to Frank. "Would you, if blease, allow associate mine for entering?"

Bud stood, frozen, quivering like a skinny white kid on the first day of high school in Compton. "Omar, you're a cop?"

"Ah Ha Ha Ha Ha Ha Ha! No, no, friend," said Omar. "My men bring you gold. We make deal now."

In half a blink, Bud was at the monitor, taking a closer look at the four men crammed into two bodies towering over a hand truck stacked with glimmering bricks. He shouted to Frank standing guard at the door, "It's okay, bro! Let 'em in."

Frank swung open the door, took a look outside, then turned around and howled, "Ho-o-ly shit, buddy-boy."

He backed up all the way to Bud's side as the behemoths tugged a gold-laden cart past the threshold.

Omar commanded, "Hassan! Sharif! Blah-la-la-la-lah," followed by a quick two-clap, causing the double-wide sentries to clear the way. With a wave of his arm, he offered, "Now for you make examine."

Bud scampered over and lifted a gold bar, turned it over several times, sniffed it, licked a corner, and held it up to the light before returning it to the pile. "Is this really ten million dollars' worth?"

"Two days ago, before loading blane, gold ten million. Now to make sure, check market." Omar's attention shifted to tapping on his phone.

Bud began a visual tally of gold bricks while counting on his fingers, but lost track when Omar reported, "Brice gold go more."

After some further calculations, Omar removed a brick and replaced it with several gold coins from a leather bag sitting atop the bars. "Now is berfect, habibi."

Bud went for a BongRite blast. After a long, slow exhale, with a tear forming in his left eye, he held up the nozzle and semi-whimpered, "But, I really don't want to sell my BongRite."

Frank glared at him, then to the gold, then back to Bud.

"But they're shiny." Bud reached out to shake hands. "And a deal's a deal, bro." He broke into the laughter of an ever-stoned dude who just sold something that cost him no more than a second-hand commuter car for ten million bucks.

Omar stuck his hand out. "Emir, Ali Bin Oyl Ghowgen shall be most pleased... since day before am married his favorite sister. Ah Ha Ha Ha Ha Ha Ha!"

Frank reached up for a high five, and Bud punched him in the stomach.

As Frank attempted to wrangle Bud into a chokehold, Omar said, "Before allow men load truck, would like for maybe burchase most excellent bus of love." He held out the leftover gold bar. "This fair brice, no, my friends?"

"I'll have to call the owner." Bud kicked Frank in the shin and broke free.

Less than three seconds later, and nearly hyperventilating while speaking, Bud said, "Hey, bro, you're never gonna believe it, but I got a guy over here that will give you a hundred-ounce gold bar for the Love Bus."

It was hard to make out what Herb screamed from his end.

Either way, Bud held the phone at arm's length until the verbal abuse stopped. And then he yelled, "No I'm not fuckin'…" but stopped mid-sentence, pocketed the phone, and grumbled, "Fuckin' dick hung up."

Frank put an arm around Omar's shoulder and smiled like a used car salesman in a room full of suckers with excellent credit. "We can work something out, my friendly friend."

# 22

The next morning, Bud stood smack dab in the middle of the kickback room, alongside a cart piled high with glittering gold. Tugging an earlobe, he muttered, "What to do – what toooo, do?"

He retrieved the leather drawstring bag resting atop the stacked bricks and bounced it in his palm. The lovely timbre of clanging coins gave him a smile. "Guess I better stash this shit."

The sack got tossed onto the stack and Bud set off down the hall, disappearing into the workshop.

Minutes later, the newly minted gazillionaire returned, clutching a medium-sized cardboard box, which he placed on the dining table. A second trip resulted in a tool bag getting delivered next to the box.

Bud dug into the bag to find the utility knife used for cutting through the box's tape. He removed a Weeble Bong from within and planted a slightly wet kiss onto its smiling glass face. "Hello, old friend."

After setting it upon the table, the Weeble Bong wobbled and he lurched to catch it. But it did not fall down. Wearing his dopiest smile, Bud said, "Forgot about that genius shit!"

Bud proceeded to unpack the five remaining Weebles, which got lined up on the table as though they were getting ready to rumble. A dropkick sent the empty box down the hallway toward the workshop. He took a Weeble to the fridge, loaded it half full of ice cubes, and then retired to the couch.

Fifteen minutes' worth of bong hits later, Bud managed to get to his feet, semi-waddled his way to the tool bag, whipped out the drywall saw, and got busy cutting open the wall next to the washing machine where the dryer had been. Before too long, a ceiling-high, rectangular piece of drywall was removed, exposing empty cavities between three studs.

A proper understanding of geometry, combined with the ability to read a tape measure, allowed Bud to determine the cavities' useable volume. He threw in a quick check of a gold bar's dimensions, with some counting on fingers, and then got to work stacking gold bars into his hollow hideaway.

Ten stacked bars later, Bud whipped out his tape measure for a double-check of used versus remaining space. His math skills led him to the numerically proven conclusion. "Right on. Break time." Numbers don't lie, so he headed for the couch to do the Dougie with his Weeble.

Not three steps into their doper's dance party, Herb entered through the workshop door, stumbled over the empty box, and screamed like a hurricane blowing through a kazoo. "Dude, I told you a thousand fucking times, don't leave shit in the hallway!"

Bud set the bong down and used both hands to whoa up the bitchy attitude. "Sorry, bro. I wasn't expecting you."

Unwilling to be reined in, Herb continued complaining and threw in a beady-eyed stare. "I didn't see the Love Bus, was hoping to have the place to myself."

"Come over here and have a smoke," Bud said. "I got some great news for you."

"No time for your bullshit." Herb flung the box into the workshop before stomping closer. "I'm just here to grab some clothes and head back to Kat's – where the idiot quotient is zero."

The discovery of the five Weeble Bongs sitting atop the table halted Herb in his tracks, where he screamed, "What the fuck, asshole? You trying to remind me how your stupidity left me bankrupt?"

"Chill, bitch," Bud said with a laugh. "You're far from broke."

"How do you fucking figure?" Herb screeched.

"We sold the Love Bus for you," Bud said. "I tried calling you back. But luckily, after you hung up on me – like a dick, I might add – Frank negotiated another forty ounces of gold for her."

"Bullshit!" Herb bellowed at the top of his lungs. "Quit fucking with me."

"See for yourself, bro." Bud waved an arm toward the kitchen. "You got a hundred forty ounces of gold on the counter."

Herb turned, stared briefly, rubbed his eyes, and then inched toward the gold hoard as if he was sleepwalking during a wet dream.

"Oh yeah, I forgot," Bud said. "There's also your share of the eighty pounds of pot pellets we sold."

Trance-like, Herb examined the gold bar and then took tally of the coins. He turned around, looking more puzzled than a pack of naked homophobic contortionists playing Twister, and spoke with a slight murmur. "Wait, tell me what's going on here."

"Remember that funny-talking hippie dude Omar I introduced you to at the barbecue?"

"Vaguely," said Herb with a slight shrug.

"Well, that dude works for some super-rich Emir," Bud said. "And he bought the Love Bus, bro."

Sounding all puppy kisses and rainbow-flavored lollipops, Herb moved toward the couch wearing the friendly smile that had taken over his face. "I'm not complaining. But why not cash?"

"Gold is money, bro!"

"Cash is way easier to deal with," said Herb.

"You can go trade yours for pieces of paper any time you want." Bud pointed at the cart laden with gold. "But before you split, gimme a hand with mine. Them fuckin' bricks are a hassle."

Herb did a fifty-yard dash, covering about twelve feet, and picked up a bar. "Where the fuck did you get all this?"

"Omar gave me ten million in gold for my BongRite." Bud grinned and snapped a bongload. "When he showed up yesterday with the coin, I got more freaked out than when you caught your mom kissing Santa Claus under the mistletoe... belt buckle!"

Herb laughed. "Fuck you."

"It's not my fault your mom blew a mall Santa." Bud winked and held up the irresistible Weeble, loaded with a bowlful of freshness. "Let's take a few rips. Then you can help me move the rest of my gold."

"Sounds like a plan, dude." Herb dropped onto the couch and reached for the bong. "Aren't you bummed to lose your BongRite?"

After a moment mulling it over for a bit, Bud smiled. "Believe it or not, I'm fully stoked to get back to old-school doobie and Weeble-Bong-hit chillin'. That smoke pump shit got way too fuckin' crazy, bro."

"You think?" Herb gave him a friendly shove. "Now you'll have to do some work every time you want to burn a joint."

"Not even," Bud said. "I'm gonna rescue me a family of chimps from the circus and teach them to roll joints. Saw that shit on YouTube."

"Sure you did." Herb picked up the lighter and sparked a bowl.

"No lie," said Bud. "And they work for peanuts."

Herb expelled a hearty hemp cloud and coughed a few times. "That's elephants."

Bud looked up from reloading duties and shook his head. "How the fuck can an elephant roll a joint, bro?"

Leaning in for a shoulder-to-shoulder nudge, Herb laughed. "You're still the same old dummy."

Bud nodded and scratched his butt. "That's ten-million-dollar dummy to you."

"Honestly, I'm glad that fucking BongRite is out of here," Herb said. "I never want to see another pellet-feeder device again in my life, even if I got snowed in at the North Pole."

Bud sighed. "Looks like we're back to canned soup."

"I'll still make you homemade soup, man."

"Thanks, bro." Bud stood up. "Help me get the rest of this gold."

"Sure thing," said Herb as he made his way to the cart. "Are all these going to fit in that space?"

"Should just about make it," Bud said. "Then I'll replace the drywall, tape the joints, and paint her up like new. First thing tomorrow, I'm gonna go buy another dryer. That'll hide it even more."

Herb took a brief survey of the room. "What happened to the dryer we had?"

"It was part of the BongRite," Bud said. "That's how I made the fuel."

Herb lugged three gold bars over and began handing them over one by one. "One does not make fuel."

Bud said, "I kinda did, bro."

"What does that even mean?" asked Herb.

"I made the hydrogen that fueled the BongRite."

"You are such a dumbass," Herb scoffed. "You were undoubtedly using natural gas."

"Nope, hydrogen, bro," Bud insisted, and laid out three fingers one at a time. "I also used it to run my buggy and the pellet cooker in the Love Bus."

"Your buggy's motor won't run on hydrogen," Herb said.

"Well, at first it wouldn't," Bud agreed. "But after I modified me a natural-gas direct injector, threw in a new cam, and did a few other tweaks – coil, plugs, timing – the hydrogen made her go real sweet."

"Impossible," Herb scoffed. "Trust me. You're just too high to know any better."

"See for yourself." Bud pointed to the top-left monitor. "That big tank just outside the rollup, its chock-full of the hydrogen that runs my buggy."

Herb moved close enough to reach out and touch the tank's image on screen. "Where'd this come from?"

"Been there for months," Bud said. "C'mon, bro, hand me a few more bricks."

Shuffling backward to the gold cart, Herb kept an eye on the monitor. "How much gas does that hold?"

"Well, it's a four-hundred-gallon tank," Bud said. "But I don't know how many pounds of gas are in it; pressure gauge broke."

Herb stood there mumbling under his breath until he gave a stern "Can't be!"

"It is, bro. Trust me." Bud gestured to the gold. "Fuck, dude, let's finish this shit. I got stuff I wanna do."

Herb wasn't listening or responding, only babbling incoherently with a perplexed expression, looking like an English bulldog with its head out a race car's window.

Bud nudged him aside and began moving gold on his own.

Ten minutes passed, and then, without even a goodbye, Herb wandered off.

Finding himself all alone, Bud turned to the monitor and grumbled, "Shit," at the sight of Herb approaching the hydrogen tank.

After looking the tank up and down, Herb examined the certification tag. Next stop, the buggy for additional scrutiny, back to the tank, and finally into the workshop, where he checked the former BongRite sites.

When he saw Herb heading back toward the kickback area, Bud scurried to the couch and got to Weebling.

With Herb half a step into the room, it was hard to tell if his shouting was in excitement or anger. "I don't know what you're trying to pull, dude."

"What do you mean?" asked Bud.

"This is a prank you and Frank are playing, right?" Herb went to the gold cart. "And these are just movie props."

"Not even, bro." Bud said. "They're more legit than Bigfoot."

"I'm pretty sure there's a logical explanation for all this." Herb threw his arms in the air and just about begged, "But why, how?"

"Well, I..." Bud paused. "Promise you won't be mad?"

"It would take a lot to make me mad right now." Herb picked up a gold bar and gave an encouraging smile-nod.

"Right on." Bud held Weeble at arm's length. "How bout a bong rip, bro?"

"For sure, man." Herb raised his voice a notch for effect. "But first I need to know what the fuck is going on here."

While avoiding eye contact, Bud spoke just above a whisper. "Remember when the dryer steam fucked up all our electronics?"

Herb scowled while nodding, but in a flash remembered to put on his fly-catching honey face. He laughed and said, "Looking back, that shit was kind of funny. Don't you think?"

Bud shook his head and continued with a bit more confidence. "Then you were being a miserable prick, and told me to vent the dryer to outside. Or you were gonna kick me out and do all the manual labor around here."

"I remember a version of that scenario." Herb took a seat and reached for the Weeble. "It's all in the past, dude. Please continue."

"Here goes." Bud paused long enough to make sure it wasn't a trick. "I never vented the dryer to the outside."

"What do you mean?" said Herb.

"It would've been a big fuckin' hassle," Bud grumbled.

"Not a problem, totally understandable." Herb smiled before snapping the bongload in one mighty pull.

Watching the guy who looked and sounded a lot like Herb had Bud shaking his head. "Dang, figured you'd be way more mad."

Herb smiled and waved smoke away. "So what if you used an indoor vent kit?"

Bud took a deep breath, followed by a full confession. "Well, I kinda designed my own indoor venting system."

"That still doesn't explain a thing." Herb leaned in close. "I am still unclear on why there's a tank full of what you claim to be hydrogen out back."

"Oh, that's easy." Bud put on a dopey smile. "Whenever the dryer ran, it split the steam in two. Then I sent the oxygen into the grow room and hydrogen into that tank."

Herb had no follow-ups; instead, he elected to stare at Bud for what felt like hours. Every so often, he'd shrug and get ready to speak, but think better of it to get back to mumble-staring at Bud enjoying bowl after brain-damaging-bowl.

His contemplation ended with a knee-slapping, hearty laugh. "You almost got me, dude." Herb bounced from the couch to make a beeline for the laundry area, where he examined the remnants of Bud's handiwork. "Tell me one more time what you claim you did."

"I got tired of having to run the dryer every time I wanted to use the EternalFlame." Bud walked over to pick up a hose lying on the ground. "So I hooked up this water supply."

"So what, there's a water hose?" Herb said.

"Well, once steady water flowed, I needed bigger and bigger tanks to store all the hydrogen I was making." Bud pointed to the wall. "See those two gas hoses? They were hooked up to my dryer-vent-splitter thingy. One goes to the hydrogen tank outside, the other to the grow room."

Herb checked the hose and then bent down to retrieve a transformer barely peeking out from behind the washer, which he shook in Bud's face. "You're telling me that you split water and recovered a four-hundred-gallon tank full of hydrogen using this tiny transformer?"

"Actually, that transformer got toasted by a lightning-strike power surge. And a minor fire." Bud sold it with a bashful grin.

"I need to research your claim much further," said Herb as he stomped off toward the workshop with transformer in hand.

Bud, apparently relieved about not being scolded, gave a friendly holler, "Right on, bro!" and went back to gold stacking.

Within the hour, all the gold bars were stacked neatly inside the wall, so Bud screwed the drywall cutout back into place and headed for the kitchen.

As Bud searched through the cupboards, Herb walked up to his side to deliver a pat on the back, along with his newest scientific theory. "It appears that in your stoned-ass idiocy, you might possibly have stumbled upon a way to separate water into its elements without using any energy source. It's a method commonly called 'water splitting.'"

"That's awesome, bro," Bud said. "Let's order pizza to celebrate."

Herb was trembling like a Chihuahua in an ice storm. "One thing's for sure, it's definitely not propane in that tank."

Bud looked sad upon discovering only crumbs remaining in a potato chip bag. After dumping them down his gullet, Bud asked, "So you're not mad, bro?"

"Not at all, dude. Quite the opposite." Herb took a deep breath and then pulled Bud in for a bear hug.

"Calm down." Bud broke the embrace and patted him on the butt. "It's not that big a deal, bro."

"Wrong, man. Efficient and economical water splitting is a huge deal." Herb beamed. "I hate to tell you, though. We would have made far more money if we patented the process and put it on the market."

"That's an awesome idea," Bud said. "I'll head to the market and grab a couple of those rotisserie chickens."

"The Emir will never put the device on the open market." Herb defaulted back to his condescending self. "We stumbled upon the 'Holy Grail,' and dummy you sold it for pennies on the dollar."

"No biggie," said Bud. "The Emir probably doesn't even give a shit about no 'Holy Grail.' Besides, I didn't sign nothing. Frank and me just loaded all the BongRiteEternalFlame shit into Omar's van."

Herb was so worked up it looked like he was slam dancing with a ghost. "That's great! Technically, legally you own all the rights. Do you think you might be able to build another EternalFlame?"

"I kinda-sorta remember how I split that shit," Bud said. "Probably could do it again in no time flat."

"That's great! Tomorrow we'll have a new dryer in need of venting." Herb dug a notepad from the drawer. "I'll start a list."

"Better put a pizza on top of that list." Bud passed him a Sharpie. "Cheese helps me think clearer."

"Anything you need, dude, just let me know!" Herb crossed the room and plopped down onto the couch. "Call it in while I load you a bowl. We need to get you back to the state you were in when you first built the BongRiteEternalFlame."

Bud stopped punching numbers into his phone, cocked his head sideways like a puppy discovering itself in a mirror, and laughed. "You're a dummy, bro. I was in California!"

# Visit Budslovebus.com
# for the Sweetest Swag
# South of Saskatchewan!!!

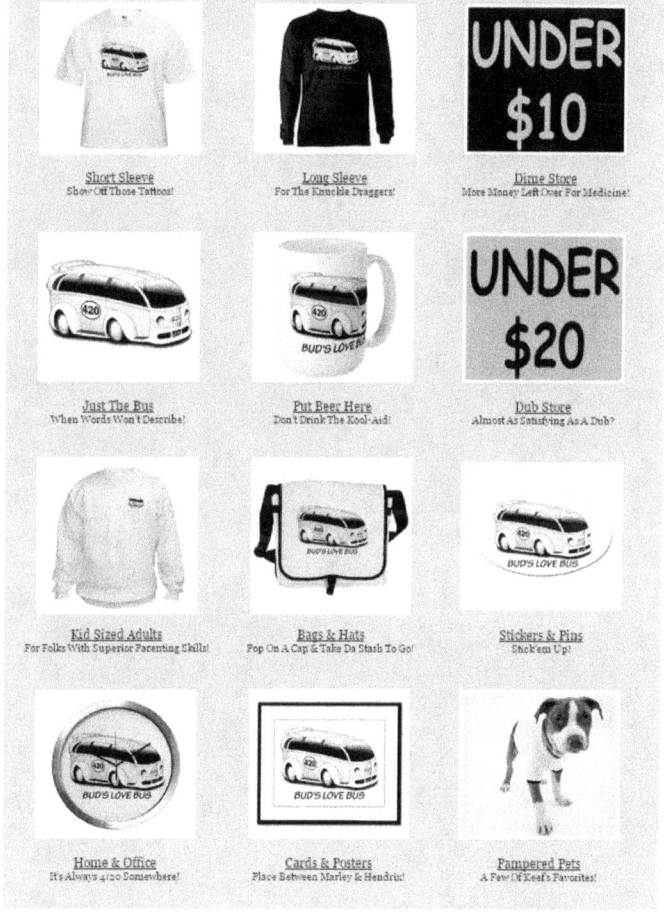

Also Sign Up To Receive **_FREE_** Prizes
& Deep Discounts on Bud Gear!

www.ingramcontent.com/pod-product-compliance
Lightning Source LLC
Chambersburg PA
CBHW072234170626
46813CB00003B/1218

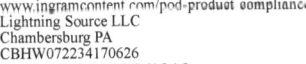